A Hairy Scary Christmas

A Spring Harbor Cozy Mystery

Amber Crewes

Pen-n-a-Pad Publishing

Copyright © Pen-n-a-Pad Publishing

First published in December 2024

All characters and events in this publication, other than those clearly in the public domain, are fictitious and any resemblance to real persons, living or dead, is purely coincidental.

Copyright © Pen-n-a-Pad Publishing

The moral right of the author has been asserted.

All rights reserved. This book or any portion thereof may not be reproduced or used in any manner whatsoever without the express written permission of the publisher except for the use of brief quotations in a book review.

For questions and comments about this book, please contact info@ambercrewes.com

ISBN: 9798304106559
Imprint: Independently Published

Other books in the Spring Harbor Series

Hair Today, Dead Tomorrow

A Short Cut to Murder

Snip Once, Die Twice

Killing Off Loose Ends

Curl Up and Die

Bangs, Bullies and Betrayal

Permed to Deadly Perfection

A Hairy Scary Christmas

A Grim Trim in a Gym

A Blonde that didn't Respond

A Spring Harbor Cozy Mystery
Book Eight

1

"On the tenth day of Christmas my true love gave to me..." Tillie hesitated, pausing as she swept the hair around Summer's station.

"Don't look at me," Summer laughed. "I only remember 'Five golden rings.'".

"Your last name is Snow, and you don't know The Twelve Days of Christmas?" Misty asked, shaking her head.

Tillie joined in. "Not much Christmas spirit for someone with your name."

Summer exaggerated rolling her eyes. "Wow, that's the first time I've ever heard that."

They all laughed, bringing Mrs. Beesley out of her office. "What's all this racket?"

"Teasing Summer about her name," Tillie said.

"What's the tenth day of Christmas?" Misty asked.

Amber Crewes

Mrs. Beesley automatically looked to Summer for the answer, but got another eye roll instead. Then she tapped her finger to her chin and scrunched her brows.

"Ten lords a-leaping," the middle-aged woman in Misty's chair said excitedly.

"Really?" Misty asked, brushing out the new long-layered style she'd just given the woman. "Like landlords? I don't think I want ten of those."

"Your last name is really Snow?" The woman in the chair was involved now, and seemed happy about it.

Summer shrugged. "Blame my mom for marrying a man with that name...then double blame her for naming me Summer on top of it. Cruel cruel joke."

"And you don't like Christmas?" The woman, clearly someone who loved Christmas—with her all-white puffy sweater, white tights, green scarf, and red berry earrings—put a hand to her mouth.

"I like Christmas just fine." Summer gestured to the new decorations around the salon. Poinsettia plants sat on every available surface—real ones! Holly and vines danced across the walls. Not to mention the giant Christmas tree by the shampoo racks. "I'm just not the authority on Christmas trivia people think I should be."

The woman opened her mouth as if to say, 'Well I am,' but stopped herself. She did, however, reposition herself and straighten her posture, which basically said the same thing. Then she checked her nice gold watch and Summer gestured for Misty to wrap up the appointment.

4

A Hairy Scary Christmas

Tillie put the broom away and set to work rearranging the shampoo bottles. Summer caught her eye and Tillie immediately let out a belabored sigh. It was clear she wanted Summer and Mrs. Beesley to hear it.

"When's your flight?" Summer asked, taking the bait.

"It was tonight, but it got pushed till the morning. My mom wasn't happy, but I told her I don't control the airlines." She continued to sigh and straighten the shelves.

Summer smiled. "You know, if you leave here early, you'll be mad at yourself. Remember?"

Tillie's sigh turned to a groan. "Yes, I remember."

"The second you put on your coat, we'll get a walk-in." Summer gestured to the empty salon, aside from Misty's client, and noticed Mrs. Beesley head back to her office. She was going to let Summer handle this.

"Maybe we should test that theory." Tillie stood and walked toward the coat rack.

"What about you?" Summer asked Misty, who was finishing up her client's 'do.

"Still staying," Misty said, but Summer couldn't read her tone. She knew the girl was homesick. They'd talked about it a lot over the past couple of weeks. But for some reason, she was determined to spend her first Christmas on her own.

It made Summer admire her more, and feel a bit of her own homesickness. "Well, if you change your mind..." Summer glanced toward Tillie, slowly inching toward the door, then back at Misty, who pulled the salon cape off of the

Christmas-loving woman. As soon as the client was up, Misty pulled her phone from her pocket and grew extremely interested in the screen.

Summer smiled at the client on her way past. "Those layers look great on you."

"Thanks," she said, fluffing the ends of her hair a bit as she beat Tillie to the door.

With the salon empty of clients, Summer slipped her phone out of her pocket. She had a text from Evan: *'How's the holiday rush?'*

Summer smiled and texted Evan back, *'Everyone's ready for vacation. Tillie's practically running out the door to get home. It kind of makes me sad I'm not going home for the holidays'*.

Even as she sent the text, she realized her parents' house was no longer home. Her last home was Atlanta, Georgia, and she was happy to be gone.

'Let me bring you some holiday cheer. I've got a new blend for you to try'

'I can't. I have a client coming'

'Lunch after?'

'We'll see. Tillie's leaving and Misty's kinda homesick. I might stay and keep her company'

'OK but we're going around to look at Christmas lights. You promised'

'If I'd known you were this full of Christmas cheer, I might not have agreed to be your girlfriend'

A Hairy Scary Christmas

'Bah humbug'

———

The bell above the door rang and Summer spun around, thinking it was her appointment, Mrs. Edwin. The Mayor's wife was already thirty minutes late for her appointment. Instead, a young woman with her hair in a loose bun shivered from the cold and hurried inside. "Do you take walk-ins?"

Summer looked behind her, knowing Tillie was long gone. Misty was already working on a client, elbows deep in hair dye. Mrs. Beesley was in the back, but Summer knew she wouldn't be thrilled to be pulled out for a last-minute haircut.

"It looks like my appointment is a no-show. How can I help you?"

"I've had a change of plans, and I'm going out of town. I'd like to do something with this," the woman said, pulling her long blonde hair down from the bun. It fell straight as a board all the way down her back.

"Your hair is beautiful," Summer said, leading her toward the shampoo area. "What were you thinking of doing?"

"Something to give it body, or else I'm just gonna have this scrunchie with me forever."

Summer took the scrunchie in question and shoved it in her smock pocket. "I'll fix you right up, and you'll be done with that thing forever." She sat the woman in the chair and turned on the warm water.

Amber Crewes

"I like the decorations, especially for a place called Summer Cuts." The woman shivered when the water touched her.

"Thank you. Some people around here like to give me a hard time about my name." Summer shot a sarcastic look over at Misty.

"What? I can't hear you," Misty replied, turning on the hair dryer.

"What are you doing for the holidays?" the customer asked.

"You're looking at it," Summer said.

"Bah humbug," came a familiar deep voice from behind her.

Summer spun around to find Evan holding two drink carriers of coffee. He raised them up over his head so they wouldn't spill as Summer wrapped him in a tight hug and tried to reach for the single cold one in the group. "Gimme!"

He lowered the drinks and Summer took a big swig of the iced coffee before choking.

"It's not caramel," he said through his deep laughter. "If you would have waited half a second, I could have told you."

Summer took another, slower drink. "Mmm, it's delicious, though. What is it?"

"I call it Holiday Cheer." He handed hot ones to Summer's customer, Misty, and Mrs. Beesley who came out to see what all the racket was.

"Awww," everyone said in unison, and Summer smiled up at Evan, assuming they were cooing over him. Then she saw it.

8

A Hairy Scary Christmas

Barney came bouncing around from behind Evan, wearing the cutest green and red sweater. All the women took out their phones, including Summer, who texted a picture to Alex with, '*Is this your doing?*'

The response was an equally adorable picture of Betty in a matching sweater, followed by a bunch of Christmas tree and present emojis.

"Clearly, you and Alex have been scheming this afternoon," Summer laughed as she also sent the picture to Aunt Clara. "What are you up to?"

"Just hanging out. Figured we'd give Mrs. Walters a break. I was thinking we-"

Summer's phone rang, cutting him off. She looked down to see Aunt Clara's name pop up. "Sorry," she said to Evan.

Summer answered Aunt Clara's call. "Isn't it the cutest thing-"

"I need your help!"

"What's wrong?" Summer asked, dropping her voice. She didn't like the tone in Aunt Clara's voice. She handed Mrs. Beesley a towel and nodded to the client with wet hair at the shampoo sink. "I'm sorry, I have to take this."

"What's going on Aunt Clara?"

"She's at it again!"

Summer didn't need to ask who or what *it* was. She knew the answer would be Cousin Fern and *no good*.

"I can't leave. I have a customer and another appointment." Then she looked at the time and realized Mrs. Edwin was

9

Amber Crewes

now forty-five minutes late. She had never been late for her appointments before.

"She better not have dyed her own hair again," Summer said under her breath.

Then, her next thought chilled her.

She better not have died.

Summer shook the thought out of her head. Nobody would kill the mayor's wife. As she hung up with Aunt Clara and rushed back to a scowling Mrs. Beesley, Summer told herself to calm down.

I'm just itching for a case to solve, even at Christmas.

2

"I think I'm jealous of Barney's Christmas sweater."

Summer blew warm air into her hands to warm up her fingers. The sun was setting as they walked in the park, enjoying the Christmas lights. Evan was beside her, and Barney was in front, pulling on his leash to sniff every new smell they encountered.

"Careful what you wish for," Evan chuckled. "For all we know, Alex is having matching sweaters made for all of us."

"It would make a cute Christmas card."

Evan wrapped an arm around Summer's shoulders, and she felt the stress of the day melt off of her. It had been busier than usual, and she wondered if they were in for a very busy few weeks leading up to Christmas.

"I forgot how pretty Christmas lights can be," Evan said as they wandered through the white lights wrapped around the bare trees in the park. "Maybe I should get some for the cafe."

Amber Crewes

"With this town's obsession with Halloween, I was expecting hundreds of inflatable Santas and blinking signs that play Christmas music. But this is beautiful."

She breathed in the cold evening air as she admired the gentle white glow around them. Her phone buzzed in her pocket, but Summer ignored it.

"Are you going to get that?"

"It's only Aunt Clara calling to complain about Cousin Fern. I'll call her later. Hey, did you notice anything strange with Misty today?"

"I thought it was just me! She seemed so distracted. What's up?"

"No idea," Summer shrugged. "I know she's homesick, but for some reason she won't tell me. She's staying in town for Christmas."

"Hmm...she's staying in town for Christmas...she's glued to her cell phone..." Evan rattled off clues, counting them on his fingers.

"What are you thinking?"

Summer loved that Evan enjoyed puzzles as much as she did. Well, almost as much. It was hard to find anyone with an obsession for mysteries like Summer's.

"Oh! She asked me about giving her a new haircut the other day."

At the time it hadn't seemed strange to Summer, but coupled with Evan's other clues, it was starting to paint a clear picture.

A Hairy Scary Christmas

"I think there's a new guy in her life," Evan announced, raising his eyebrows to ask Summer if she agreed.

"Exactly what I was thinking. But it's strange. She's usually so open about her relationships."

"A mystery man," Evan chuckled. "Maybe that's the next mystery for you to solve."

"Maybe..."

Figuring out who Misty might be involved with was certainly intriguing, but there was another mystery that Summer couldn't shake from her head. Every time she tried to relax, she remembered that uneasy feeling she had carried with her all day. Margaret's missed appointment.

Her phone buzzed, startling her. Aunt Clara again. Summer silenced it.

"Are you alright?"

"Sorry. I was just thinking about something."

"Care to share?"

She didn't know what Evan would think about her suspicions. After all, it was totally normal for people to forget about their hair appointments, especially during such a busy time of year.

"I had a client miss an appointment today. I'm a bit worried about her."

"Who was it?"

His voice was filled with compassion that instantly made Summer relax. Of course, Evan would understand her.

Amber Crewes

"Margaret Edwin."

"The Mayor's wife?"

"Exactly. She's never missed an appointment with me. Not since I saved her hair on the first day I met her."

Evan squeezed her hand in his, reassuring her.

"I'm sure it's nothing. This time of year, it's easy to forget things. I almost left the house without shoes this morning!"

"That's because you leave before the sun's up," she laughed.

Evan was right. Margaret probably told her assistant to reschedule, and the girl forgot. There had to be a normal explanation for it.

For the third time in ten minutes, Summer's phone buzzed in her coat pocket.

"Maybe you should answer," Evan said. "It seems important."

"She wants to make a plan for Cousin Fern," Summer sighed.

"A plan? What for?"

"She's been running card games in the lounge at the Manor House Inn."

"What's wrong with cards? A little canasta never hurt anyone."

"Not just *playing*. She's playing for money and collecting bets from other people. She's practically running her own casino in that place."

Evan laughed and shook his head.

14

A Hairy Scary Christmas

"Good old Cousin Fern."

"The owner isn't happy. Aunt Clara thinks we need to find somewhere else for her to live."

———

Barney pulled hard on his leash, dragging Summer forward. Evan put a hand on the leash to help hold him back.

"Whoa, Barney. What's the rush?"

The beagle pulled them to a colorful sign sticking into the ground. It was out of place among the tasteful decorations that otherwise adorned the path.

"What's that?"

Barney began to dig around the sign, kicking up dirt and the dusting of snow on the ground. Summer called him back to the path.

"The Spring Harbor Decorating Contest," Evan said, reading the red and green block letters.

"I didn't know the town had a decorating contest! Can the salon join in?"

"Sadly, no. It's for residential houses."

"But barely anyone has decorations up," Summer said, replaying her morning drive to the salon in her head. Only a few of her neighbors had bothered with lights. Most places didn't go much further than a wreath on the door.

"Yeah, almost no one participates."

Amber Crewes

Evan and Summer continued their walk, curving around the last bend in the path that would bring them back toward the salon and their cars.

"But this town loves holidays!" Summer said. "Why isn't every house lit up like a Christmas tree?"

"It's sort of turned into a competition between three or four houses. I think people got tired of the same people winning every year. Actually, the Mayor's wife takes it really seriously. I could definitely see her missing a hair appointment over that contest!"

"Mystery solved," Summer laughed, and knowing this about Margaret did make her feel a little better.

"But don't let it discourage you. I'm sure we could make your apartment a winning house if you wanted to."

"Where would we put the lights?"

Summer pictured her small apartment with the shared entryway.

"You have a balcony! Think of how many lights we could wrap around those railings."

She had to admit the thought of decorating her new home was appealing, but she certainly wasn't about to join a contest when she only had a balcony to decorate.

"Some lights sound nice," she admitted. "But I wouldn't dream of taking away Margaret's trophy. Besides, the salon's way too busy these days."

"Holiday rush. I hope you're taking a break for Christmas."

"A few days," Summer nodded. "What about the cafe?"

A Hairy Scary Christmas

"Closing down from Christmas to New Year's. I haven't had a vacation all year, so I decided it was a good time for everyone to have a break."

"And your Christmas plans?" Summer asked, pushing her shoulder playfully into his arm.

"I was hoping to spend it with someone special."

Summer felt a surge of warmth through her chest as Evan bent down and gave her a sweet kiss on the cheek. It felt so nice to have someone to spend her holidays with. It made her think of Aunt Clara and those unanswered text messages.

"Would you mind if we made a party of it?" Summer asked. "We could invite Aunt Clara and Carl. And, of course, Alex and Betty."

At the sound of his sister's name, Barney's head swiveled up to look at Summer, making everyone laugh.

"We can't leave Barney without a friend for Christmas," Evan said. "Of course, it should be a party. But I notice you left Cousin Fern off that list..."

"Not intentionally!" Summer cried, realizing her mistake. "I know she drives Aunt Clara crazy, but I have to say I'm gaining a fondness for that woman."

"If Fern's there, at least we know the party won't be boring!"

"Definitely not," Summer agreed. "But we might need to tell everyone to hold tightly to their wallets. I might invite Misty too. If she doesn't have somewhere else to be, that is!"

"Will we all fit in your place? You know I love it, but it's pretty small."

Amber Crewes

"It will be cozy," Summer said, thinking of her apartment filled with laughter and Christmas Carols playing from the stereo. "Though I'll need your help with some decorations."

"My pleasure," Evan said. "And while we're at it, we'll decorate that balcony of yours too."

"If you insist."

Summer and Evan stepped out of the park and back toward the salon, where Summer's car was waiting outside.

"Aunt Clara will help with the food. She'll claim she doesn't want to, but I guarantee she'll hardly let anyone else into the kitchen the whole day. I'll ask her about it."

Summer pulled her phone out of her pocket, excited to share the Christmas party with her aunt. But when she took out her phone, she was shocked to see how many times Aunt Clara had texted or called her.

"What is it?" Evan asked, seeing how white Summer's face had gotten.

"Something's wrong," Summer said. "Something other than Cousin Fern."

3

"Is everything alright?"

Summer held the phone to her ear as her heart beat hard. Her mind began to race with all the things that could be wrong.

"It's alright," Aunt Clara assured her. "I'm sorry to call so much."

"Is Cousin Fern okay?"

"Cousin Fern?" Aunt Clara asked, and for once she seemed surprised to hear about her cousin. "Oh yes, she's fine. Or, at least, I haven't heard about any new scandals."

"Good," Summer said. She nodded at Evan, letting him know that everything was alright. "So what's up?"

"I'm wondering if you've seen Margaret Edwin today."

"No," Summer said. Just when she was starting to relax, a cold dread spread across her body. "Why do you ask?"

"It's probably nothing."

Amber Crewes

"What is it, Aunt Clara?"

"Well, I haven't heard from her. And she was supposed to meet me this afternoon at the Manor House. She was going to try to talk some sense into Cousin Fern, since nothing I say seems to be working. But she didn't show."

"She had an appointment at the salon today."

"Yes, that's what her assistant said! I called her when I started to worry."

"But she didn't show."

"What?"

"She didn't show up for her appointment. I should have called her, but we had walk-ins all day, and I was slammed. I just figured she forgot."

"That's what I thought too," Aunt Clara said. "That she forgot we had plans. But now I'm starting to worry."

"Me too. If she didn't show up to her morning appointment and she didn't meet you this afternoon, when was the last time anyone saw her?"

Summer saw Evan's eyebrows raise when he heard the words.

"What's going on?" he asked, stepping closer.

"Margaret had plans with Aunt Clara this afternoon," she said.

"And let me guess, she didn't show up?"

Summer switched the phone to speaker so Evan could be part of the conversation.

A Hairy Scary Christmas

"Aunt Clara, I have Evan here with me, too. You're on speaker."

"Hey Evan," Aunt Clara greeted warmly. "Did you hear we have a missing woman on our hands?"

"Hey now, I don't know if you should jump to conclusions like that. After all, she's a busy woman."

"What do you think could have happened?" Summer asked into the phone, ignoring Evan's warning. "Did you hear anything?"

"There's always town chatter," Aunt Clara said. "The mayor's wife is always going to be a target for gossip."

"Anything substantiated?" Summer asked. It was Evan who interrupted things, bringing both women back down to reality.

"Alright, you're getting ahead of yourselves. Let's at least wait until the woman's been gone for more than eight hours before we jump to conclusions."

"I guess that's fair," Summer nodded. "I think I'm itching for a case to solve."

"You have other things to distract you," Evan reminded her. "Weren't you calling to invite Aunt Clara to Christmas dinner?"

"Of course!" Summer put a grateful hand on Evan's arm, thanking him for the reminder.

"You're making *dinner?*"

"Well, I might need some help," Summer admitted. "But I

Amber Crewes

want to host Christmas at my place. You and Carl are invited. Oh, and Henry too!"

Summer saw Evan's eyes grow round, clearly surprised to hear her invite yet another person to dinner. But Summer didn't care if they were squeezed in like sardines. They would make it work.

"Of course, we'll be there," Aunt Clara squealed, and Summer imagined her pressing a hand to her heart in excitement. "But I think you should leave the cooking to me."

"You got it," Summer laughed. She knew her aunt far too well.

"What about Cousin Fern? Should we leave her at the Manor House to swindle the Christmas guests out of their presents?"

"She's invited too," Summer laughed. "We'll take turns keeping an eye on her."

———

"You're still thinking about Margaret, aren't you?"

"Maybe I should try to call her. If we go back to the salon, I can find her number in our appointment book."

"We're at your house," Evan said as he pulled up in front of Summer's apartment. "Just try to put it out of your mind for tonight."

Summer knew he was right. It wouldn't do any good to obsess over Margaret when they wouldn't have any more information until the morning.

22

A Hairy Scary Christmas

Evan grabbed the pizza from the backseat and walked with Summer toward her apartment. She was suddenly starving, and they sat down immediately to dig into the sausage and peppers that they both loved.

It was when she moved on to her second piece that Summer took stock of the kitchen they were sitting in.

"How am I going to cook a whole Christmas meal in here? I don't even have enough chairs!"

Evan shrugged as he took a sip from his beer.

"We'll sit on the couch. Or we can have a picnic. It will be fun!"

"Let's hope all the guests have the same attitude."

Summer stood up, thinking about each closet in her house. Where did she put the Christmas decorations?

"Where are you going?"

But Summer didn't stop to explain. She crossed into her bedroom and to the back of the closet, where she had shoved a number of boxes. She was grateful to her past self, who had carefully written the word "Christmas" across the front of one.

"You don't have to decorate right now," Evan laughed, but he saw determination in Summer's eyes.

"Christmas is a week and a half away," she explained. "I might as well take stock of what I have."

She opened the cardboard box and was quickly disappointed. It was only about half full, with some seasonal pillow covers to put on the couch pillows, a few snowman figurines, and a garland of pinecones and jingle bells that had seen better days.

"We'll go shopping," Evan suggested. "I'll get lights for the cafe and we can get some things for the apartment. We'll have this place looking like Christmas in no time!"

"Tomorrow?" Summer asked. Now that the party was real, she was feeling the pressure.

"It's a date," Evan said. He gave her a kiss and grabbed his coat.

Summer walked him to the door.

"Please don't spend all night worrying about the party," Evan said. And just as Summer opened her mouth to speak, he said, "Or Margaret either."

"You know me too well," Summer said. "I'll try."

"Good. See you tomorrow."

As soon as Evan left, Summer went back to the sad box of Christmas ornaments. Maybe if she put these out she might feel better about things. Summer crossed to the kitchen to look for tape she could hang the Christmas garland with. But her eye fell to her closed laptop.

Just a quick search, she thought.

Summer grabbed her glass of wine and crossed to the couch, the box of ornaments still open on the coffee table. She tucked her legs underneath her and opened her computer.

Where are you, Margaret? She thought as she typed Margaret Edwin's name into the computer.

A Hairy Scary Christmas

There were many hits. Spring Harbor might be a small town, but the mayor and his wife were local celebrities. Summer scrolled through pictures of Margaret at charity events beside her husband. She found articles about Margaret's clothing drive for local children. And she learned about Margaret's passion for volunteering at the animal shelter.

She looks so...normal.

Summer scrolled down, searching for anything negative or suspicious about Margaret Edwin. She learned that her maiden name was Jones, and that she had married Stewart Edwin when she was twenty-two, right out of college. She even found Margaret's high school yearbook. But still, nothing raised red flags for Summer.

Nothing on Margaret, she thought as she paused to sip her wine. *But what about Stewart?*

It felt a bit dangerous to do an internet search on the mayor, but Summer took a deep breath and hit the enter key. Article after article appeared alongside touched-up headshots and photographs. It appeared Stewart liked to show himself off as a younger man, despite the fact he was now in his late 50s.

One particular blog article caught Summer's eye. It wasn't from an established news source, so Summer knew she had to be cautious. After all, people could post anything on the internet without consequences. But the headline was too shocking to be ignored.

Rumors of infidelity plague Mayor Edwin's re-election campaign.

Amber Crewes

Infidelity...

Summer remembered Aunt Clara's words about town gossip. Could this be what she was referring to?

Summer's phone buzzed on the table next to her, making her jump. She realized how dark it had gotten outside and checked the clock to see it was nearly 9pm. Alex's name appeared on the screen of her phone, and Summer picked it up.

"Hey there," Summer said. "Did you get my text?"

"That's why I'm calling," she said. "I wanted to ask you what I can bring!"

Summer picked up her glass of wine and carried it into the kitchen for a refill.

"I'm pretty sure Aunt Clara's going to insist on cooking," Summer said. "But she might let you help."

Summer settled into the couch to talk with her friend.

Margaret will show up.

This was what Summer told herself as she closed the computer screen beside her. But even as she laughed along with Alex about Christmas plans, she couldn't shake the feeling that something was wrong.

26

4

"You mean no one's heard from her?"

Misty stood next to Summer, clipping the dry, dead ends of the woman in front of her. The girl, Jessica, was in her twenties, with hair that fell to the middle of her back. Despite Summer's efforts, she always forbade them from doing anything to the long, straight locks except trimming the ends.

"My mom called the house all night," Jessica said. "And then she called all of her friends."

"I heard the police have been called," said the middle-aged woman in Summer's chair, her hair full of foil for the blonde highlights Summer was applying.

"What about the mayor?" Summer asked, remembering her research from last night.

"What about him?"

"What do you know about him? Any reason to think he might know something?"

Amber Crewes

"What are you all talking about?"

Mrs. Beesley popped out from the back room, her voice dripping with judgment that made Summer shrink. All four women fell silent.

"Margaret didn't show for her appointment yesterday," Summer said, easing her way into the conversation. She knew Mrs. Beesley had great respect for the mayor and his wife, and she wouldn't approve of gossiping.

"Really."

Mrs. Beesley's eyebrows furrowed in concern. Maybe they were right to be nervous...

"Did you hear from her?" Misty asked.

Mrs. Beesley looked up from her distracted expression.

"I'm sure she forgot," she said, and then she rushed back to the office, but at the last minute, she turned back. "You shouldn't be gossiping."

Even the woman in Summer's chair smirked at Mrs. Beesley's scolding. Summer decided to change the subject to keep the peace in the salon.

"So you're really not going home?" She asked Misty as she folded the final piece of foil on her client's head. She glanced over to see Misty occupied by her phone, typing away.

"I know that look," Misty's client teased, looking at Misty in the mirror. "Who are you messaging?"

"What?" Misty asked, feigning innocence.

28

A Hairy Scary Christmas

"You've been far too obsessed with your phone lately," Summer said. "Who are you talking to?"

"A friend."

"Oh, come on, you'll have to give us more than that."

Jessica spun herself around to look directly at Misty. Suddenly, the three women surrounding her were waiting for an explanation.

"It's just someone at the station," she sputtered. "I'm asking if he knows anything about Margaret."

"A cop," Jessica said, her eyes growing wide. "You're dating a cop?"

"Who said anything about *dating*?" Misty asked, but Summer noticed she couldn't keep herself from smiling.

"Is that why you're staying in town for Christmas?"

"Didn't Mrs. Beesley just tell you all to stop gossiping?" Misty asked. She shoved her phone back in her pocket, trying to end the conversation.

"Why so secretive?" Jessica asked.

Misty ignored the question and spun Jessica's chair back to the mirror. Then she pulled Jessica's long hair up, letting the ends fall to her shoulders.

"Just take a look," she said, nodding toward Jessica's reflection. "We could take off a bit of length and it would frame your face so beautifully."

"You're changing the subject."

"I could even put in a few layers."

29

Amber Crewes

"No, thanks." Jessica slipped forward, letting her hair fall from Misty's hands. She stood up and pulled off her own salon cape. "Thanks for the trim."

Misty went to the front desk to take Jessica's payment, leaving Summer and her client alone. Summer started to hum along to the Christmas carols playing over the salon speakers.

"I've heard some things."

"What was that?" Summer asked. She was checking the foil around the woman's face to make sure the color wasn't over-saturating. But Ellen's words made her freeze.

"About the mayor."

Her voice was quiet, almost a whisper, and Summer leaned in.

"I don't think it was a very happy marriage."

She remembered the blog post she read last night. Had Ellen heard the rumors about infidelity?

"What have you heard?"

At first, Summer thought Ellen wouldn't say anything. She sat silently, chewing the inside of her mouth.

"You didn't hear it from me," she finally said. "But Mayor Edwin has a wandering eye..."

She wanted to ask more, but Misty was already back to clean up her station, and Ellen swiftly changed the subject.

"And what are *your* holiday plans?" she asked, as if they were in the midst of a very different conversation.

A Hairy Scary Christmas

"I'm having a few people over to my apartment," she told her. "If you're really staying in town, Misty, you should come."

"That sounds nice. I'll definitely take you up on that."

"Good."

Summer thought about all the text messages and Misty's decision to stay in town. Like Jessica, Summer was pretty sure she knew what was going on.

"And you should bring your new boyfriend."

She smirked at the shocked expression on Misty's face.

"How did you...?"

"Come on, Misty. All the clues are there—this one was a pretty easy mystery to solve."

———

Summer waved to Ellen as she pushed through the door, beaming over her new highlights. It always brought Summer such a sense of pride to see her clients so happy.

"We made it," she sighed, delighting in the empty salon.

Summer sank down in the chair at the reception desk and leaned back, giving her sore feet some relief. She and Misty had been going non-stop since 8 am this morning.

"Thank goodness we scheduled ourselves a lunch break."

Misty finished tidying her station and untied her apron before wiping her hands on her jeans. She crossed to the coat rack.

Amber Crewes

"I think I'll take a walk to the deli. Do you want something?"

"Get it delivered," Summer suggested. "Aren't your feet ready to fall off?"

"I'm alright. Besides, the cold air will wake me up a bit."

She wondered if Misty had plans to meet up with her special someone for lunch. It could certainly explain her energy right now. But Summer was too tired to tease her anymore.

"Turkey Club, please."

Misty nodded and went to the back to get Mrs. Beesley's order.

"Be back soon."

Misty practically skipped out of the salon as she wrapped her scarf tightly around her neck. It made Summer laugh to see how much energy she had.

With Misty gone and Mrs. Beesley in the back, the salon was quiet. Holiday music still played over the speakers, but Summer paused the playlist, letting the wonderful sound of silence waft over her.

She sighed and leaned back in her chair. It would be so nice to close her eyes for a moment...

Her phone buzzed in her apron pocket and Summer jumped. She looked down at a text from Aunt Clara.

I convinced them to let her stay. But she's on her last warning.

A Hairy Scary Christmas

Aunt Clara had gone to the Manor House Inn this morning to talk to the owner. After Cousin Fern's antics, he wanted her to move out.

Thank goodness! And Cousin Fern agreed to behave?

She knew it was hard to get Cousin Fern to agree to anything. She could only hope the threat of losing her housing would be enough to keep her in line for a bit. At least until the new year!

She's a stubborn thing. I'll need to keep my eye on her.

Summer felt a pang of guilt. Aunt Clara had been dealing with this Cousin Fern drama alone. The salon had been all-consuming these days, but it was no excuse for Summer to ignore her family.

I'll help too. You aren't on your own with her.

I know I'm not. But there's no reason it should take up both of our lives.

Still, I want to help.

Of course. The more eyes on the woman, the better!

The bell over the door rang and Summer looked up.

"That was fast!" She said, but then she saw that it wasn't Misty with the sandwiches. It was Alex, with both dogs trotting happily in front of her.

"Oh my gosh, look at them!"

Summer squealed as she saw the dogs in brand-new Christmas sweaters. These were blue, with smiling snowmen on them. She dropped down to her knees to scratch the pups behind the ears, thrilled to see them.

Amber Crewes

"What a nice surprise. A doggie visit is exactly what I needed on this crazy day."

Summer stood up with a smile, ready to thank Alex for bringing them by. But the look on her face stopped Summer in her tracks. Her smile faded as dread washed over her body.

"What is it?"

As if she could sense trouble, Mrs. Beesley came out of her office. She crossed to Alex with a serious expression on her face.

"Then you didn't hear?" Alex asked, looking between Summer and Mrs. Beesley. Summer shook her head slowly.

"Margaret," Summer said. It wasn't a question. As soon as she saw Alex's face, she knew it was what it must be about.

"It's Margaret."

"Is she alright?" Mrs. Beesley asked.

Alex shook her head and swallowed before delivering the news.

"She's dead."

5

"What happened?"

"She was found in her car."

Summer ushered Alex to the waiting area where they all took a seat.

"And you're sure she's dead?" Mrs. Beesley asked.

Alex nodded.

"It's all over the news. Mayor Edwin reported her missing, and the police have been out searching. About an hour ago, they found her car behind a craft store. With her body inside."

"I knew something was wrong. It's not like her to miss her appointment."

The bell over the door rang, and Misty returned empty-handed.

"Did you hear?" She asked. She joined them in the waiting area, her face white with shock.

"Alex told us."

Summer watched Misty's face, wondering if her 'friend' at the station was the one to tell her. But if the story had broken on the news, it was likely all anyone at the deli was talking about.

Mrs. Beesley grabbed the remote and turned on the TV. Since Summer took over the salon, they rarely turned it on. She always found music to be classier background noise. But they had never gotten around to taking the television off the wall.

"Our top story of the hour: Margaret Edwin has been found dead this morning. She was the 54-year-old wife of Spring Harbor's mayor, Stewart Edwin. Mrs. Edwin was reported missing early this morning by her husband, though sources said the Mayor asked the police chief to keep things quiet until they had more information."

"What does that mean?" Misty asked, outrage in her voice. "Was he trying to hide something?"

"Maybe he didn't want to embarrass her," Mrs. Beesley offered. "In case she turned up on her own."

"A 54-year-old woman doesn't drop off the face of the earth for no reason," Alex said. "He had to know something was wrong."

They turned their attention back to the news report.

"Police and firefighters had been searching for Mrs. Edwin since the early hours of this morning, covering Spring Harbor and neighboring communities. At approximately eleven thirty this morning, her car was found parked in an alley behind Spring Harbor's craft store. It was there that the police discovered her body. At this time, police do not believe there is reason to suspect foul play. Mrs. Edwin appeared to die of natural causes."

Natural causes?

Summer didn't believe it for a second. Margaret was a healthy, active woman.

"They're not telling us the full story. Misty, what are the cops saying?"

Misty raised her eyebrows.

"How should I know?"

"I thought you had a *friend* over there. What did he tell you?"

"I know as much as you do," she insisted.

The news report started repeating the same information. Summer reached over to turn the volume down. They wouldn't learn anything new from listening to the same report over and over again.

"What are you thinking?"

Alex knew the look in Summer's eyes. Her friend would be running through all the possible scenarios in her mind.

"I think the police should be looking a bit closer at the man who reported her missing."

"Mayor Edwin?"

"I did some research last night and found something interesting."

"If you're going to start with that town gossip, I'm leaving."

Amber Crewes

Mrs. Beesley stood up.

"Then you know about it?"

She hesitated, torn between going back to her office and giving away what she had heard.

"This is Margaret," Summer reminded her. "We've seen her every two months for nearly a year. If you've heard something, don't you owe it to her to tell us?"

She saw Mrs. Beesley wavering.

"People always want to take down a powerful person..."

"What did you hear?" Misty asked.

Mrs. Beesley looked from woman to woman. Finally, she plopped down into a chair.

"Cheating. They say there were...problems in their marriage."

"Who was cheating?" Alex asked. "Margaret or the Mayor?"

"Of course, the mayor!"

Mrs. Beesley seemed offended that Alex would even ask.

"But there's nothing proven. Only town whisperings to try to bring the man down. No one ever came forward to substantiate it."

"I don't know," Misty said, twisting a strand of hair around her finger. "It's a pretty small town. It would be hard to hide an affair with someone."

"Exactly," Mrs. Beesley said, as if this proved that it had to be false.

A Hairy Scary Christmas

"Unless you work with them every day in the same office," Summer suggested. All eyes spun around to look at her. "From what I heard, Mayor Edwin was having an affair with his assistant."

―――――

"Have you heard?"

Evan pushed through the door to find the four women discussing theories about the case.

"Yeah. It's all over the news," Alex said. She gestured to the TV screen.

Christmas lights flashed across the screen and Summer realized they were showing Stewart and Margaret's house. She turned up the volume.

"Margaret Edwin was an enthusiastic participant in the Spring Harbor Decorating Contest. She has taken home the prize for best decorations five times in the last seven years, much to the dismay of the other participants."

"How sad," Misty sighed. "She won't get to show off her Christmas lights this year."

"Residents of Spring Harbor have already begun discussing ways to honor her memory this holiday season," the news story continued.

The news cut to a shot of people being interviewed outside the diner. Summer recognized one of her clients on the screen.

"I really can't believe she won't be here for Christmas," the woman said tearfully. "It was her favorite holiday. I wasn't

Amber Crewes

going to decorate my house this year, but I think I'll get some lights in honor of Margaret."

The news continued to show individuals committing to putting up Christmas lights in Margaret's name.

"We should do that," Alex said. "It's a nice way to remember her."

"I was just telling Summer I wanted to get some lights," Evan said. "Maybe a new mystery will be the push she needs to actually do it."

Summer smiled at Evan's joke, but she was distracted. It was nice that people were thinking of ways to honor Margaret, but why wasn't anyone talking about how or *why* she died? Surely the town wouldn't accept a label of 'natural causes'.

She pulled out her phone as the group began discussing how to further decorate the salon and Evan's cafe. Summer began searching her phone, hoping that new information might have appeared about Margaret's death or even the Mayor. If someone was posting blog articles about the Mayor's infidelity, maybe there was someone on the inside who had information about the murder. Because murder was exactly what Summer thought this was.

"Earth to Summer—are you with us?"

She looked up to see Evan leaning close to her.

"Sorry. I'm just not ready to accept that this was an accident. Doesn't it seem suspicious to you?"

"But the police don't suspect foul play," Misty insisted.

40

A Hairy Scary Christmas

"Do you have confirmation of that?" Summer asked. Misty hesitated. She knew Summer was wondering if she had heard any inside information from her new boyfriend. After a moment of thought, Misty slipped her phone out of her pocket and found a number. She stepped away to make the phone call.

"You think Mayor Edwin's infidelity caught up to him?" Alex asked.

"But those rumors have existed for years," Mrs. Beesley said. "What changed now?"

"Maybe she found out?" Summer thought out loud.

"He's up for re-election this year," Evan said. "Maybe she threatened to talk."

This new theory held a lot of weight, and everyone nodded.

"That sounds like motive to me."

Summer flipped through her phone to confirm that Stewart Edwin was at the end of his term in office. For a man who enjoyed all the perks of being a small-town mayor, he might do anything to keep his position.

"I don't have much," Misty said as she returned to the group.

"Anything helps," Summer assured her.

"They're telling the public 'natural causes', but not everyone at the station believes that."

"Really?"

"They're giving this a full investigation. If there's any foul play, they'll find it."

41

Amber Crewes

"Well, that's something," Alex said. "At least the police are looking into it."

Summer nodded, but she didn't feel any better about things. She knew the police had gotten things wrong in the past. She also knew the chief of police worked very closely with Mayor Edwin.

"I'm going to take a walk."

Summer stood up and grabbed her coat from the rack.

"You have an appointment in half an hour!" Mrs. Beesley told her.

"I'll be back."

"Do you want me to come?" Evan asked, helping Summer into her jacket.

"I'll be fine. I'll swing by the cafe on my way back. I think I'm going to need some caffeine."

"I'll have it waiting," Evan assured her.

"Don't forget the appointment!"

Mrs. Beesley called through the door as Summer left. But she had already forgotten about all the clients she had stacked up this afternoon. There was a mystery to solve, and Summer knew that if anyone was going to get to the bottom of this, it had to be her.

6

As soon as Summer climbed out of her car, she caught Sheriff Brady's eye. And he was glaring at her.

So much for flying under the radar.

The Sheriff mouthed something that looked remarkably like 'Go Away'. He even flapped his hand at her as if shooing away a fly.

Luckily for Summer, the scene of the accident was swarming with people, and Sheriff Brady was quickly distracted as he spoke to one of his officers. Summer counted three different news crews reporting on the accident. Then there were Spring Harbor citizens, pushing into the police tape to try to get a glimpse of whatever was happening.

Summer scanned the scene as she slammed the car door closed.

Amber Crewes

They were behind the craft store, but this wasn't just an alley filled with dumpsters. Sure, there were dumpsters along the brick wall of the building, but there were also parking spaces on the other side of the roadway. Summer guessed it was where employees from all the stores in this shopping complex parked.

So she parked her car here. Or someone else did...

The blue Honda was neatly tucked into a parking spot, with no tire marks on the ground and no damage to the vehicle. It was no wonder it took the police so long to find her. Nothing at all looked amiss about the little car sitting peacefully in the row of parked cars.

Police tape was arranged in a square around the scene. The news cameras were right in front of the car, trying to get a good camera angle. Summer walked along the side of the tape, moving closer to the car. She hid herself behind a tall SUV where she could look through the windows at the action.

"No cuts or signs of injury."

One of the deputies was speaking with Sheriff Brady. Was he the one who found her?

"But there was something around her mouth. Like maybe she had been sick, but it looked more like foam. Like a dog with rabies or something."

"Don't compare the Mayor's wife to a dog, Jacobs," Brady warned. "Especially not around the cameras."

"Of course. Sorry. I've just never seen anything like that in a human."

A Hairy Scary Christmas

Summer remembered the news reports that kept repeating the words 'natural causes'. Foaming at the mouth certainly didn't seem natural to Summer. She remembered Misty's friend in the police station saying some of the police didn't believe the story. Summer had to agree with them.

"Keep this to yourself," Brady warned the deputy. "The coroner will run a full toxicology report. If there's foul play here, we'll find it."

At the mention of the coroner, Summer scanned the crowd, hoping to see Trish Dockett there. Sure enough, she saw Trish surveying the scene, making notes in her notepad, and asking the crime scene photographer to take pictures.

When Sheriff Brady and the deputy walked away, Summer walked from around the SUV to stand against the police tape.

"Trish," she called, trying to keep her voice down in case Brady was still in earshot.

The coroner didn't look up, and Summer had to repeat herself. This time, Trish Dockett looked over. When she saw Summer, she gave a shake of her head, but she walked over.

"Why am I not surprised?"

"I'm not here to cause trouble," Summer assured her. "But everyone's saying this was natural causes. We can't let this get swept under the rug. If someone is responsible for this, we need to hold them accountable."

"We don't *need* to do anything. Let the police do their jobs."

"The police work for the mayor," Summer whispered.

Amber Crewes

She saw Trish's expression change. It was slightly shocked and filled with warning.

"Be careful, Summer. It's dangerous to make those sorts of accusations."

"Hey, what's going on here?"

Summer looked up to Sheriff Brady striding toward them. His face was red in frustration.

"Sorry Sheriff," Summer called. "Was just inviting Trish to my Christmas party."

She turned around before Brady could call her on her bluff. Summer strode back to her car, feeling even more certain that she needed to look into Mayor Edwin.

'Meet me at the Cafe.'

Summer sent off the text to Aunt Clara before starting up her car and driving away.

––––––––

"Look at you!"

Aunt Clara slid into a chair across from Summer, wearing a motorcycle jacket and gloves. She smirked at Summer as she pulled the gloves off her hands, tugging one finger at a time.

"Do you think Carl will get the hint?"

"You're asking him for a motorcycle?" Summer asked. She had to shake her head at Aunt Clara, who never ceased to surprise her.

46

A Hairy Scary Christmas

"I've been hinting at it for six months. Now that I have the outfit, I need the vehicle to match."

"But aren't you a little…"

"Stop right there."

Aunt Clara put up a hand to silence Summer.

"Alright," Summer laughed. "No comments on your age. But I only want you to be safe. I don't know if I could handle taking care of Cousin Fern on my own."

"And how are my two favorite ladies?"

Evan set down two coffees in front of Summer and Aunt Clara. Ice coffee for Summer, and a mocha for Aunt Clara.

"Aunt Clara's setting the bar for Christmas presents this year. She's asking Carl for a motorcycle."

"That's a big gift," Evan chuckled. "Let's hope you don't give Summer any ideas. I'm only a struggling cafe owner, after all."

"Oh, don't worry. Summer is far more practical than I am. Besides, Carl can afford it."

"By mortgaging his house?" Evan joked.

"Not at all. Remember that little card game Cousin Fern was running?"

"Aunt Clara…"

Summer grew instantly suspicious. She had a feeling she wouldn't like what she was about to hear.

"Let's just say I made sure he was the lucky winner that

Amber Crewes

night. He won't have any problem covering the pre-owned motorcycle I've picked out."

Summer shook her head as Evan chuckled.

"Don't encourage her," Summer scolded him. "No wonder Cousin Fern keeps coming up with schemes."

Aunt Clara lifted her mocha to her mouth and blew across the top before sipping it. She simply shrugged, showing Summer she didn't have a response to this accusation.

Evan shared a look with Summer that said: 'She's your family'.

"I have to get back to work," he said. "But tell me. Did you learn anything at the scene?"

"What scene?" Aunt Clara asked, suddenly leaning forward. "Did you go down to the crime scene?"

"Keep your voice down. I don't need the whole town knowing I'm investigating this. At least not yet."

"So, you think it was a crime? I *knew* those reports of natural causes were suspicious."

"I don't know anything yet. But it's clear Sheriff Brady and the coroner have a lot of questions."

"They suspect foul play?"

A crash sounded from behind the counter. They all looked to see Evan's employee mopping up a mess of spilled coffee across the counter. Evan left the table to go assist with the spill.

"Tell me everything you learned," Aunt Clara encouraged.

48

A Hairy Scary Christmas

"Margaret was a good person. If someone harmed her, we owe it to her to figure out who."

"First, I need to ask you a question. You mentioned hearing rumors about Mayor Edwin. Did they have to do with infidelity?"

Aunt Clara gave a slow but definitive nod of the head.

"So, you've heard?"

"Mrs. Beesley heard the rumors too. And one of my clients the other day. It sounds like it was an open secret around here. Do you think Margaret found out?"

"I'm not sure."

Aunt Clara sat back in her chair, looking off in the distance as if she were remembering something. "I remember a group of us tried to tell her once. But she wouldn't let us get it out. She really loved him."

"Something could have changed. Maybe the Mayor had to keep her quiet."

"It seems risky. And why kill her in her car? It's too complicated."

"Can you think of anyone else who would want to harm her?"

Summer was keeping notes on her phone about the case, and she clicked to the spot that said 'suspects'. So far, Mayor Edwin was the only name on the list.

"Everyone loved her," Aunt Clara shrugged.

The yellow cursor on her phone blinked at her. They had nothing.

49

Amber Crewes

"So, we have one suspect and zero motives."

Summer closed her phone with a sigh. This mystery was proving to be harder than she thought.

Her phone lit up with a text from Mrs. Beesley.

'Where are you?'

"I have to run," Summer said, jumping to her feet and throwing her coat on. She glanced at the clock to see she was fifteen minutes late for her afternoon appointment.

"Let me know if you hear anything," Aunt Clara cried out.

"I will. And good luck with Carl."

7

"Have a good day, Barney."

Summer scratched the dog's ears as the smell of freshly brewed coffee wafted to her nose. Evan stepped over to them and bent down with a treat. Barney instantly turned away from her to devour the small cup of whipped cream he held out.

"You spoil him," Summer laughed as Barney got whipped cream all over his nose.

"And his mom," Evan said. He handed her an iced caramel latte topped with her own whipped cream treat.

"You're the best," she smiled. Summer stood up as Evan brought Barney behind the counter. She knew he would have a nice day relaxing in Evan's office, likely being fed far too many treats.

"See you tonight."

As she turned to leave, she nearly ran into Sheriff Brady and another officer coming through the door.

Amber Crewes

"Sorry," she mumbled. But as soon as she recognized the Sheriff, she knew she couldn't miss the opportunity to ask him some questions.

"Sheriff Brady," Evan called from the counter. "The usual?"

"You bet," he said. "And whatever Deputy Mason wants."

The Sheriff gestured to the man standing next to him. Summer didn't recognize him, and she was about to ask if he was new to the force when Evan did it for her.

"A new recruit?" Evan asked. "What'll you have?"

He caught Summer's eye, and she knew he was doing some detective work of his own.

"Black coffee," the man said with a nod of thanks.

"Deputy Mason moved to the area a few months ago," Brady explained. "We're lucky to have him in our small town. He's used to big cities and the crimes that come with them."

"Welcome." Evan handed two steaming paper cups of coffee across the counter.

Summer saw her opportunity, and she stepped closer.

"Is there any news on the Margaret Edwin case?"

She saw the corner of Brady's mouth turn up in a rueful smile.

"I was wondering when you were going to ask."

"The news said she died from natural causes, but she wasn't even sixty years old. What's natural about that?"

A Hairy Scary Christmas

"Deputy Mason, meet Summer. One of the town's most... inquisitive residents."

Summer rolled her eyes at Brady's description of her, knowing that he didn't mean it as a compliment.

"If someone is responsible for this, the town should know about it."

"Look, you'll find out, along with everyone else."

It was clear Brady was losing patience, but Summer didn't care. Getting to the truth was more important than dealing with Brady's attitude and rude remarks. As Brady and Mason turned to leave, Summer called out after them.

"I'm trying to help you. We don't have to be on separate sides."

She saw Brady's shoulders stiffen, and then he turned around. The look on his face could melt snow.

"I'm not sure what makes you think you're a part of this investigation," he said carefully. "But I'm here to tell you that you're no more important than any other resident in this town. You will find out when the rest of the town does."

"And what about all the cases I helped you solve?" Summer asked. She made sure she looked directly at Mason as she said it, wanting the new guy to know exactly how much she had helped with the previous investigations.

"You were helpful," the sheriff admitted, though Summer could tell it was difficult for him to say. "But this case is... high profile. It will take more than some amateur sleuthing to find answers here."

With that, the sheriff turned and left the coffee shop.

53

Amber Crewes

"At least he admitted it's a case," Summer shrugged, smiling with Evan. She knew she had ruffled the sheriff's feathers a bit and she hoped she had reminded him of why he might need her.

"I'm sorry about that."

Summer looked up at Deputy Mason in front of her. He was a tall guy with shaggy brown hair and kind eyes.

"He shouldn't have spoken to you like that."

"Don't worry about it," Summer said. "Sheriff Brady and I have a...unique relationship. Eventually he'll see he needs me on this case."

Mason nodded goodbye and turned to leave, but Summer followed him out the door, sensing another opportunity.

"Is there anything *you* can tell me?" she whispered.

They both eyed Sheriff Brady, who was waiting in the police car for Mason.

"Look, I just started at the station. It wouldn't go well for me if I said anything."

"Right. I understand."

Summer nodded as Mason crossed to the cop car. She made a point of waving at Brady as she crossed the street toward the salon.

———

"Summer, come quick."

54

A Hairy Scary Christmas

Misty and Mrs. Beesley were standing under the TV, watching the news. Summer rushed through the door and set her coffee on the check-in counter as she joined them to listen.

"Police are now saying that the death of Mrs. Margaret Edwin may not be natural after all. New evidence has come to light from the coroner's office that makes the cause of death inconclusive."

"You were right," Misty whispered, her eyes round in shock.

Summer glanced at Mrs. Beesley, who was dabbing her eyes with her sleeve. She was pale, clearly distraught at thinking her friend might have been murdered.

"At this time, the police have not named any persons of interest in this case. This means that Mayor Stewart Edwin is not currently being investigated. Police say Mayor Edwin is cooperating with them and has offered to give them anything they need to solve this case."

"I can't believe it."

Mrs. Beesley dropped down to a chair in the waiting area and began to cry. Summer grabbed tissues from the counter and brought them to her as Misty rubbed her back.

"It's so sad," Misty said. "She was such a nice woman."

"I can't imagine why anyone would want to hurt her," Mrs. Beesley sniffed. "Everyone loved her."

Summer remembered Aunt Clara telling her the exact same thing yesterday. It seemed like everyone she spoke to had the same impression of Margaret: she was not a person anyone would want to harm.

55

Amber Crewes

"What if Margaret wasn't the target?"

It wasn't the first time Summer had considered this. She remembered researching the Mayor even before Margaret's body was discovered. When she found nothing suspect in Margaret's background, she had started to think Mayor Edwin might be the real target.

"You think someone was trying to hurt the mayor?"

Misty was shocked by the idea, but Mrs. Beesley seemed almost comforted by it.

"It would make more sense," she said, holding the tissue to her eyes. "Maybe someone didn't agree with his politics. Or maybe..."

Her voice trailed off, and Summer wondered if Mrs. Beesley was thinking about the affair with his assistant.

"She was found in a blue Honda. Do you know if they shared the car?"

"Don't you remember?" Misty asked, suddenly lighting up. "Last time she was in, she was dropped off in that black town car. She was embarrassed about it because she said she didn't like to ride around in the Mayor's car. It made her feel too pretentious."

"That's right." Summer stood up and started pacing, trying to pull the memory out of her head. "She said Mayor Edwin was visiting his mother or his sister—I can't remember. But he drove the Honda."

"Leaving Margaret with the chauffeur."

"So, they both drove the Honda," Mrs. Beesley said, putting

A Hairy Scary Christmas

the pieces together right along with Summer and Misty. "Maybe someone thought he was driving."

"It's very possible," Summer said.

She watched Misty pull her phone from her pocket and send off a text. It appeared Misty's obsession with her phone was continuing. She had a guess about who she was talking to.

The trio sat in silence for a moment as the news showed the footage of Margaret's house decorated with Christmas lights. They had run through all the new information they had, so they were re-using the same stories from yesterday. Once again, they talked about Margaret's love for Christmas and her winning decorations.

"We should get to work," Mrs. Beesley said, pulling herself together. She sniffed hard as she stood up.

Misty didn't seem to hear Mrs. Beesley, even when she walked directly in front of her to cross back to the office. Instead, Misty stayed glued to her phone, typing away with both thumbs.

"Who are you talking to?" Summer asked.

Misty startled and quickly shoved her phone into her back pocket.

"No one. We should get to work."

She rushed to her station to begin preparing for her first client.

What's with all the secrecy?

Amber Crewes

Summer clicked off the news and pulled up the Spotify account on the computer. She turned on the Christmas music and heard "Jingle Bells" through the speakers. Then she moved to the front window and plugged in the Christmas lights.

Murder might be on her mind, but Summer knew a gloomy hair salon was bad for business. It was time to put aside the mystery for a few hours and focus on her clients.

8

"Who's ready for some decorating?"

Summer ran a cloth along her counter and tucked her hair scissors into the drawer. She smiled at Evan as she closed her station for the night.

"Hey, where's my dog?"

She looked at Evan's feet, expecting Barney's happy greeting. But he wasn't in the salon.

"Alex swung by to pick him up. She said she and dogs were working on a special project."

"Well, that's not at all suspicious."

Summer laughed as Evan wrapped an arm around her shoulders to give her a hug of greeting.

"It's a ghost town in here. Where is everyone?"

"Misty ran out around four o'clock. She said she had a date to get ready for."

"Wow. She must be really excited about this guy. And Mrs. B?"

"She's been hit pretty hard by Margaret's death, so I told her to go home after lunch. That was after she tried to charge a client $400 for a trim. Luckily, we caught it before she swiped the credit card."

Evan grabbed Summer's coat from the rack and helped her into it. He wrapped her scarf around her neck, playfully covering her face with the warm plaid fabric.

"Hey!" she laughed, pushing the scarf down so she could see. Evan's goofy smile cheered her up, and she realized how happy she was to see him.

"We have to hurry if we're going to get to the hardware store before it closes. Should I turn these off?"

As Evan crossed to the Christmas lights surrounding the large salon window, Summer felt a surge of sadness. It didn't feel right to turn those off after everything that happened.

"Leave them on. I know how much Margaret loved Christmas lights—it will be the salon's tribute to her."

"Won't Mrs. B complain about the electric bill?"

Normally, Mrs. Beesley would be the first one to turn her nose up at something frivolous like that. However, after Margaret's passing, Summer felt she would actually appreciate the gesture.

"You let me worry about that," Summer smiled.

They crossed into the cold, windy night, and Summer locked the door to the salon. The hardware store was only a

A Hairy Scary Christmas

few blocks away, so they walked arm in arm toward the historic building. As they walked, Evan told her the hardware store had been passed down in the same family for generations. It was the oldest building in town.

"Welcome to Sanders Hardware."

Summer smiled at the sixty-something man with a long, white beard behind the register. She couldn't help wondering if he made extra income playing Santa at Christmas parties. He was a perfect replica of the holiday figure.

"Hey, Mr. Sanders," Evan waved. "I know you're closing soon. We'll be quick."

"Take your time, son. It's Christmas after all."

The earthy smell of wood permeated the old building, which looked like a converted barn. They walked across wide-plank floors and through old wooden shelves to find the Christmas decorations section.

"We might have been too late."

The shelves were nearly empty, with only a few boxes of Christmas lights or holiday garland still on the shelves. A woman in her sixties was browsing the options as well, her arms already holding three boxes.

"It must be because of Margaret," Summer guessed. "Everyone's eager to honor her. It seems like the whole town loved her."

"Excuse me." The woman who was next to them was now cutting in front of them. She snatched the last box of white

Amber Crewes

Christmas lights that was right in front of them, nearly pushing Summer out of the way to get to them.

Summer glanced sideways at Evan, noting the woman's aggressive behavior as she struggled to balance the many boxes in her arms.

"I guess we're going with colored lights," Evan chuckled. He pulled a few boxes from the shelves, reaching around the woman to claim them before she could snag them.

"Are you competing in the holiday decorating contest?" Summer asked, telling herself to be kind. It was Christmas, after all.

The woman stared at her and only pulled the boxes closer to her chest as if she were worried Summer was about to steal them.

"Are you?" The woman asked pointedly.

Summer tried to place the woman, wondering if she had ever seen her in the salon. She had short, blonde hair that was tight on the sides and puffy on the top. Summer's fingers itched as she imagined taking some length off the top to give her a sleeker, modern look.

"I don't have a big enough place," Summer told her. She held out her hand, but quickly realized the woman had too much in her arms to be able to shake.

"I'm Summer."

The woman only stared at her before turning around and storming away.

A Hairy Scary Christmas

Just as Summer and Evan finished choosing their items, they heard an angry voice coming from the front of the store.

"It said $7.99. I saw it on the shelf."

It could only be the woman they had just seen in the Christmas aisle, who was now checking out.

"This is the 500-count outdoor light set," Mr. Sanders answered calmly. "It's $34.99. It may have been in the wrong place on the shelf."

"That's not my fault."

Summer and Evan came around the corner with their arms full. Despite the limited options, she found lights for her balcony, a four-foot Christmas tree on sale, and some seasonal decorations to put up around the house. Mr. Sanders even had a section for placemats and napkins, and they found a nice holiday set on sale.

"For Barney?" Evan asked.

He held up a mini stocking with a cute snowman on the front.

"If you get one for Barney, you'll need one for Betty, too."

"Done."

Evan grinned at her even as his stomach let out an audible grumble.

"Someone's hungry," she teased. "Let's get out of here and get you some dinner."

They walked toward the check-out, where the older woman was getting increasingly agitated.

Amber Crewes

"If you advertise a price, you have to honor that price."

"I'm sorry, Mrs. Cole. We've had many people in here for Christmas lights today, and things get moved around on the shelves. Look right here on the box—it says the price clearly."

Mrs. Cole scowled as Mr. Sanders pointed out a sticker on the top of the box. She clearly wanted to keep arguing, but there was irrefutable proof of the true price.

"Let me offer you a 30% off coupon for those lights. We sent one out in this week's coupon flyer."

Mr. Sanders found the coupon and scanned it for her.

"There. It brings your total to $56.96. Will that work for you?"

Mrs. Cole scowled at the register, acting like the price offended her. She opened her wallet and began thumbing through her bills.

The Santa lookalike glanced at Evan and Summer and gave them a small smile. It was clear he was trying to apologize for the wait. Summer waved her hand, letting him know they weren't in a rush, though Evan's stomach might say otherwise.

"Here."

Mrs. Cole thrust three twenties at him, and he checked her out. He carefully packed her items into a bag and handed her the change.

"Happy Holidays."

A Hairy Scary Christmas

Summer half expected the woman to shout back a 'Bah Humbug'. But she simply grunted and stormed out of the store.

"I guess there's no pleasing some people," she said as she and Evan dropped their items onto the counter.

"I'm used to it with Mrs. Cole. Though she seems to get grumpier and grumpier every year."

"Who is she?" Evan asked. "I don't think I've ever met her."

There were dog treats at the register, and he grabbed two and placed them among their items as Summer playfully rolled her eyes.

"Wanda Cole," Mr. Sanders said. "She lost her husband almost twenty years ago."

"How sad." Summer suddenly felt guilty for being annoyed at the woman.

"Ever since it happened, she's stayed in her house. She gets her groceries and supplies delivered so she can come into town as little as possible."

"But she's getting Christmas lights."

Summer and Evan shared a look, both wondering the same thing: Did Wanda Cole know Margaret?

"Ever since Margaret's passing, I can't keep lights on the shelves. Everyone wants to honor her memory."

"It's very nice of the town," she said. "And Mrs. Cole."

"It is. Though I feel a bit guilty profiting off of the woman's death."

Amber Crewes

Summer paid for her items, grateful for the extra clients she had these past few weeks. It meant she could cover this Christmas haul with her tips.

"Okay, you're all set. You have a good night now."

Mr. Sanders passed a bag across the counter with a smile.

"Thanks for staying open for us."

Evan and Summer waved as they headed to the door.

"Let's grab some dinner," Evan suggested. "If I don't get some food soon, I'll start chewing on these dog biscuits."

9

"Alex and the dogs are curled up on the couch watching Christmas movies."

The image made Summer smile as she pushed her phone back into her pocket. Knowing Barney was doing well, Summer and Evan pushed into 'Little Italy', the cute Italian restaurant in town. They had walked over from the Hardware Store, so Evan still carried the Christmas lights and decorations.

"I have no idea when we'll be able to put these up," Summer commented. "We're both so busy at work right now."

"Two please," he said to the hostess.

"Maybe Aunt Clara will take pity on me and come over to help before the party."

"Or Cousin Fern," he suggested. "It might give her something productive to do."

They were led toward the back of the restaurant, where the

Amber Crewes

fire from the pizza oven spread warmth around the tastefully decorated room.

"Summer?"

She looked at a booth along the wall and saw Misty waving at her. She had a large plate of Alfredo in front of her. Then Summer saw the man sitting across from her: it was the deputy she met at the coffee shop this morning.

"Deputy Mason," Summer whispered as she and Evan crossed to say hello.

"Her mystery man," Evan whispered back in surprise. "Of course it's him. How could we miss that?"

Summer should have known the new deputy she met this morning was Misty's 'friend' at the police station.

"Hi Misty. Hi Deputy Mason."

"Oh, so you know each other?" Misty asked, full of glee. Summer only had to look at her to know how happy she was. Any worry Summer had about her mysterious new boyfriend melted away.

"We met at the cafe this morning. Poor Deputy Mason had to put up with me grilling him about the Margaret Edwin case."

"I wouldn't say you were grilling me."

"What would you call it?" Evan chuckled. After all, he had watched Summer interrogating the man.

"I'm always happy to talk to an interested citizen," Mason said kindly.

68

A Hairy Scary Christmas

"Summer's more than a citizen," Misty assured him. "She's solved more cases around here than the whole police force put together."

"Well, I wouldn't go that far."

"Don't be modest, Summer. I'm surprised they haven't deputized you by now."

"I try to do what I can."

Summer was flattered by Misty's praise, but she wanted to be careful. Sheriff Brady resented her for solving his cases and getting involved. She didn't want Deputy Mason to feel the same way.

"The more people working on a case, the better. That's what I say."

"I'm relieved to hear you say that."

Evan put a hand on Summer's arm.

"We should let them enjoy their dinner. If we don't order soon, I'm going to dive into Misty's Alfredo."

Summer knew Evan was hungry, but she also knew she wouldn't have many chances to speak with Deputy Mason alone. Maybe he would be more forthcoming without Brady here.

"Is there anything you can tell an interested citizen?" she asked. "Any new developments in the case?"

Summer saw Misty and Mason share a look across the table.

"I really can't," he told her. "I'm sure you can appreciate that it's a high-profile case. The department has to be tight-lipped."

Amber Crewes

"Of course. With the mayor involved, I'm sure it's complicated."

"Exactly. With an election next year, we have to be careful not to influence the results one way or the other. It's a delicate balance."

"Then you think this was related to the Mayoral race?" Summer asked, full of excitement. It felt like she had gotten something out of Deputy Mason, after all.

He looked down at his spaghetti and meatballs, and for the briefest moment, Summer wondered if he might say more. But then he straightened and looked back at them.

"Like I said, I can't divulge any information."

Summer and Evan said their goodbyes and crossed to their own table.

"You just can't help yourself, can you?" Evan said as he shook his head. Summer smirked at him.

"Stop teasing and eat something."

She nodded to the basket of bread on the table. Evan's eyes grew round, and he quickly grabbed a breadstick. With one bite, it was half gone, and Evan leaned back in his chair, finally satisfied.

———

"He's sort of by-the-book, don't you think?"

Evan and Summer waved goodbye to Misty and Mason, who had finished their meal and were now heading out of the restaurant. Summer watched Mason

A Hairy Scary Christmas

help Misty with her coat and offer his arm to her as they left.

"I think he's good for her," Summer said. "He's the opposite of who I would expect for Misty, which is exactly what makes him a good fit."

"She certainly seems happy."

Summer agreed. It was wonderful to see Misty so excited about someone new. She finally understood why Misty had decided to stay in town for Christmas.

Summer took a bite of her side salad, reminding herself there was more on the table than the amazing pumpkin ravioli she had already half finished. Evan was halfway through his chicken dish.

"It's interesting he brought up the election."

"I guess they think the accident must be related. Could someone be targeting the Mayor?"

"Misty, Mrs. Beesley, and I wondered the same thing. Did you know they shared a car? Maybe someone thought the Mayor would be driving."

"But there's nothing to indicate the car was tampered with."

"I know. That's what I can't figure out. Unless the police aren't telling us something."

They chewed in silence for another minute while Summer worked through the possibilities. She knew the Mayor was popular in town. He was favored to win re-election. Did someone think the only way to win was to take him out?

"Who else has announced they're running?" she asked.

71

Amber Crewes

"There's an older man in town who runs every year. Asher Roades. But he knows he won't win. He's a volunteer at the animal shelter, and he only uses it as an opportunity to raise some money for the shelter and get some animals adopted."

"Now that's a cause I can get behind."

"Ellen Avery is a more serious contender. She ran four years ago, and people were surprised by how close the race was."

"She almost won?"

"I wouldn't say that. Mayor Edwin was the clear winner, but she did develop a strong following."

"And she's running again?"

Evan nodded as he used a breadstick to soak up the sauce on his plate.

"Her face is plastered on billboards all over town. Haven't you seen those commercials?"

Summer shook her head. They rarely had the television on at work, and lately, she had been far too tired in the evenings to turn anything on at home.

Evan fished his phone from his pocket and searched. When he found what he was looking for, he handed the phone across to Summer.

She saw a middle-aged woman with curly brown hair cut severely across her shoulders. Her brown eyes were scowling out of the screen even before Summer hit 'play'.

"Spring Harbor deserves a mayor who upholds family values."

A Hairy Scary Christmas

A deep-voiced narrator was speaking while images of Ellen Avery flashed across the screen.

"A mother who knows what's best for our children and a public servant who won't keep secrets from the community."

Suddenly, an image of Mayor Edwin flashed across the screen. They had found some unflattering pictures of him, scowling or pointing in an aggressive manner. Then there was a shadowy image of a man on a dark street, his collar pulled up to block his face.

"Mayor Edwin has a secret. He isn't being honest with the citizens of Spring Harbor."

A final image of Ellen Avery came on the screen. She was standing behind a folding table with trays of food, spooning something onto a plate while she smiled at the hungry person. Her name flashed across the bottom of the screen as the narrator concluded:

"Choose Ellen Avery. A candidate with decency."

Summer handed the phone back to Evan.

"Wow. It's bold to accuse the sitting mayor of hiding something."

Of course, Summer thought immediately of the Mayor's infidelity. Was that the secret Ellen Avery was referring to?

"There are always going to be rumors floating around," Evan said. "I never put much stock in them."

"For someone who runs a coffee shop, you are remarkably uninterested in the town gossip," she teased.

Amber Crewes

Evan shrugged.

"I guess I like to make my own decisions about people."

"Okay, then what's your decision on Ellen Avery?"

Evan thought for a moment as he popped his last piece of chicken into his mouth.

"That she doesn't like Mayor Edwin. And she might do something drastic to bring him down."

10

The next morning, Summer was alone in the salon with Mrs. Beesley. It was Misty's day off, so it would only be the two of them today. As Summer watched Mrs. Beesley tidy magazines in the waiting area, she wondered how she was handling Margaret's death.

"Busy day today," Summer said as she reviewed their bookings.

"Mm-hmm."

"We won't have any space for walk-ins."

Mrs. Beesley nodded but didn't respond.

Maybe I should give her space.

Summer crossed to her station, where her phone lit up.

'Meet for lunch? We still need a plan for Cousin Fern.'

'Absolutely. I'll have an hour at 1pm.'

'Perfect. Meet me at the diner.'

Amber Crewes

'The diner? What about the cafe?'

Their usual lunch spot was at Evan's place. Summer liked it because she could say hello to her boyfriend during the day. And Aunt Clara liked that they usually ate for free.

'I have a hankering for a tuna melt.'

Summer shook her head at the screen.

'See you at the diner.'

She and Aunt Clara were certainly overdue for a larger conversation about Cousin Fern and her living situation, but Summer hoped they would also talk about Margaret. If she knew Aunt Clara, she would be talking to everyone about Margaret now that the death was considered suspicious. Summer hoped she had some new leads to follow.

"Do you think I should have told her?"

Summer looked up from her phone to Mrs. Beesley right next to her.

"What?"

"Do you think I should have told Margaret about the rumors? About the...infidelity."

"Oh, Mrs. Beesley. Are you feeling guilty about that?"

"I can't stop wondering if things would be different. Maybe this could have been avoided."

Summer saw tears pool in Mrs. Beesley's eyes.

"You can't do that to yourself. We don't know what

76

A Hairy Scary Christmas

happened yet or *why* it happened. And it certainly wasn't your fault."

"She was my friend. I should have said something."

"From what you told me, you didn't even believe those rumors yourself."

"I didn't. But now that this has happened, I can't stop wondering."

Summer put a hand on Mrs. Beesley's shoulder. It was upsetting to see how affected she was by this.

"Are you sure you're alright to be here today?" Summer asked, even though she knew she wouldn't be able to handle all the appointments by herself. Still, it might be better to turn people away than to have a tearful Mrs. B cutting their hair.

"I'm fine."

Mrs. Beesley sniffed and stepped back so Summer's hand dropped from her shoulder. She seemed to drop into herself again, disappearing into her thoughts as she continued preparing for her first client.

Perhaps a change of conversation would do some good.

"Do you know a woman named Wanda Cole?"

The name definitely surprised Mrs. Beesley out of her thoughts.

"It's been years since I've heard that name. Poor thing lost her husband, and it just about destroyed her."

"We had a run-in with her at the hardware store."

Amber Crewes

This brought a chuckle from Mrs. Beesley, who shook her head.

"Let me guess—she was...less than friendly?"

"She was. I tried to introduce myself, but she wasn't very interested in conversation."

"That sounds like Wanda. She used to be a social butterfly around town, visiting all the shops and getting into everyone's business. But all that stopped when her husband died suddenly. Now she stays at home, not talking to anyone. I'm surprised she was shopping."

"Did she know Margaret?"

Mrs. Beesley thought for a moment, casting her mind back a few years.

"I do think they were friends. And they both participated in the Holiday Decorating Contest. I think the two of them even helped start that competition in the first place."

"It's nice she's going out of her way to honor Margaret," Summer noted. "Are you putting lights up this year?"

Mrs. Beesley scowled, and Summer saw a flash of the old Mrs. B. She held back a smile.

"Oh, no. It's too much for me. I can't be up on ladders or climbing trees—I might break my neck."

"Well, if you want any help, let me know. It sounds like the whole town will be lit up for Christmas this year."

The front door chimed, and Summer looked up at their first client.

"Welcome to Summer Cuts! You must be our 9 am."

A Hairy Scary Christmas

Summer walked to the front to check the woman in. She was young, probably early twenties, bundled up in a coat and wool hat.

"I'm sorry, I don't have an appointment. I was hoping you might be able to squeeze me in."

Summer's stomach dropped. She hated to say no to people, but their schedule was packed to the gills already.

"I'm sorry. We're completely full today. But if you'd like, I can take a look at tomorrow."

"Oh, please!"

She heard desperation in the woman's voice. The woman pulled the winter hat off of her head. Her shoulder-length blonde hair had a green tinge that was noticeable from Summer's position several feet away.

"Please? I can't look like this for Christmas."

"You tried to dye it yourself?" Summer asked.

The girl nodded, as if she couldn't bring herself to say the words.

"Alright," Summer sighed. "Come on back."

———

The morning was a whirlwind of appointments, with Summer and Mrs. Beesley bouncing back and forth from the shampoo sinks to dryer chairs to their hair-cutting stations. Despite her earlier sadness, Mrs. B was a wonder, working on her own clients and even helping with Summer's.

Amber Crewes

"You're all set. Have a great holiday."

Summer pulled the hair cape from the woman's shoulders. She felt pride as the woman ran a hand through her hair and beamed at her reflection. She walked the woman to the door and caught a conversation between two women in the waiting area.

"I think it was the assistant."

"You think she took her out to have the Mayor all to herself?"

An added benefit of the day had been all the talk about Margaret. Summer had been uncharacteristically quiet, letting the individuals in her chair guide the conversation. They inevitably talked about Margaret.

"I'm ready for you, Mrs. Palmer."

Summer guided the older woman back to the chair and asked what she wanted to do today. After discussing a touch-up of her highlights and a trim, Summer got to work.

"I hope you don't mind me asking, but I heard you talking about the Mayor's assistant."

"It's not a secret, dear. Everyone knows that man was running around with that girl."

"Girl?" Summer asked. "I heard she went to work at the Mayor's office after graduate school."

"It's just an expression, dear. Sure, she might be in her twenties, but that doesn't make her appropriate for a married man who's almost sixty."

80

A Hairy Scary Christmas

"Certainly not," Summer agreed. She had a feeling Mrs. Palmer was someone who liked people to agree with her. Summer waited, hoping Mrs. Palmer would continue.

"That girl clearly has political ambitions."

"Why do you say that?"

"Why *else* would she get involved with a married man?"

"Right."

Summer forced herself to hold her tongue. She knew there were many reasons people found themselves in relationships, but she wasn't going to disagree with Mrs. Palmer.

"So, you think she's responsible?"

"Who *else*?" the woman asked.

"But why take out Margaret? It seems like things were going well for her. What changed?"

"Margaret found out, of course. She was going to expose them."

Summer stopped mid-cut. This was new information she hadn't heard before.

"Are you sure? How do you know that?"

"Angela Robbins. She was Margaret's best friend. She found Margaret crying one night. When she asked what was wrong, she said she knew about the Mayor's assistant. *Elizabeth*."

Mrs. Palmer hissed the assistant's name as if merely saying it could bring bad luck.

81

Amber Crewes

Summer tucked the name Angela Robbins away, knowing this was someone she would need to track down to corroborate this story. She wasn't ready to take the word of Mrs. Palmer, who seemed prone to exaggeration.

"Let's get you over to the dryer so your color can set."

Summer deposited the woman in the dryer seat and took a breath. Mrs. Palmer was her last appointment before lunch, so she grabbed her phone and checked in with Aunt Clara.

'What do you know about the Mayor's assistant, Elizabeth Jenkins?'

Aunt Clara responded immediately.

'I'm way ahead of you.'

'What do you mean?'

'Elizabeth Jenkins picks up the Mayor's lunch at the diner every day. And guess who's going to be there when she does?'

'Us?'

'Exactly. I think it's time the town got some answers.'

'I like how you think.'

She had wondered why they weren't eating lunch at the cafe. Now she knew Aunt Clara had something more than lunch on her mind.

82

11

When she pulled up to the diner, it was impossible to miss the police car parked across the street. She stepped out of her car and saw Deputy Mason sitting in the cop car, window down despite the chill in the air. Summer raised her hand in a wave, and Mason nodded at her.

He's a tough guy to read.

At dinner with Misty last night, he had seemed so friendly, but now he was back to his formal self. It was like once he had the uniform on, all personal relationships went out the window.

When she looked toward the diner, she saw Aunt Clara waving feverishly through the large window. She was sitting in a booth with a good view of the parking lot and the full street. But it wasn't Aunt Clara's enthusiastic waving that took her by surprise. It was the other person sitting with her.

"Cousin Fern," Summer said as she slid into the booth. "What a surprise."

83

Amber Crewes

"Your Aunt thinks I need a babysitter."

Fern sat with her arms crossed, looking like a petulant child. Summer eyed her aunt for further explanation.

"She was taking bets on who would win the Christmas Lights competition. Right in the lobby of the Manor House Inn. I had to bring her along before the owners found out."

"Cousin Fern," Summer sighed. "You know you can't be doing that."

"No one was going to find out," Fern insisted. "Your Aunt is just overly cautious. Which is a bit surprising for someone who benefited so handsomely from my card game."

"Oh, right," she said. "Carl's money for the motorcycle."

Summer remembered Aunt Clara's comment about making sure Carl won big so he could cover the Christmas present.

"She has a point," Summer said, but Aunt Clara only rolled her eyes.

"So now you're on *her* side?"

"No sides," Summer insisted. She decided to drop the accusations and simply enjoy the company of her family members. "I'm glad you're here, Cousin Fern."

"Thank you, dear. Now tell us what you've learned about the case."

Clara and Fern looked at her eagerly, desperate to soak up all the details about the mayor's wife. Summer should have felt bad that they were so excited about another death in town. After all, she really liked Margaret. But Summer had to admit these conversations thrilled her as well.

84

A Hairy Scary Christmas

It must run in the family, she thought.

"There was a lot of chatter at the salon about Elizabeth, his assistant. Some people think she's responsible."

"That little slip of a thing?" Aunt Clara asked. "Unlikely. Besides, if the rumors are true, they've been in a relationship for years. What changed?"

They paused to give their orders to the waitress, and as soon as she stepped away, the three women leaned close again to talk.

"Mrs. Palmer thinks Margaret found out about the affair."

"Found out? How does Mrs. Palmer know that?"

"She said her friend found her crying one day."

"Oh, come on," Fern burst out. "I cry all the time. That doesn't mean she knew about her husband's affair."

"Don't worry, it's on my list to follow up," she assured her. "I'm not in the habit of trusting all the gossip that comes through my salon."

Summer glanced out of the window, where Deputy Mason was still sitting in his car. He sat with his arm hanging out of the open window, his gaze stuck on the diner.

"Did you notice the Deputy out there?"

"You mean Sheriff Handsome?" Cousin Fern asked. "How could you not?"

Summer ignored Fern's comment, only rolling her eyes as she continued.

"What do you think he's doing out there?"

85

Amber Crewes

"Maybe the same thing as us. I don't think Elizabeth Jenkins killed Margaret, but she's an important person to talk to."

"Which is why you're stalking her lunch spot."

"Why *we're* stalking her," Aunt Clara said, raising her eyebrows. "Don't act like I'm alone in this."

"Now I understand why she brought me," Fern mumbled. "She needed an accomplice."

———

"Hey, look."

Summer saw a young woman in a tight suit and tall heels walking toward the diner. She held a scarf tight around her neck and a purse that looked more expensive than any bag Summer had ever owned.

"That's her," Aunt Clara said, confirming Summer's suspicions.

Elizabeth Jenkins was a tall, thin woman with a long nose and round blue eyes. Her hair was piled on her head in a messy bun, but blonde curls escaped and hung around her face.

"Those heels look far too uncomfortable for a day at the office."

Summer had to agree with Cousin Fern. Poor Elizabeth looked like she was wincing with each step she took.

"Don't do anything drastic," Summer warned as Elizabeth pushed her way through the door and into the diner.

A Hairy Scary Christmas

"Hey Shelly," Elizabeth said. "Is Mayor Edwin's order ready?"

"One minute, hon. They're wrapping it up now. Take a seat."

Elizabeth glanced around the very full diner. It was impossible not to notice that most of the guests in there were staring directly at her.

"Would you mind bringing it outside when it's ready? I'll just be right in the parking lot."

Elizabeth turned and headed for the exit, away from all the stares.

"Excuse me."

Summer was on her feet before she knew it, blocking the door before Elizabeth could get to it.

"I wonder if I could ask you some questions."

The young woman's expression grew dark and suspicious.

"I'm sorry, but I'm not speaking with anyone. If you have questions for Mayor Edwin's office, you can take that up with the press office."

She stepped forward and reached for the door, but Summer moved with her. She hated to be so pushy, but this might be her only chance to speak to Elizabeth. She needed to convince her she was on her side.

"Look, I don't want to cause you any trouble. I just want to know your side of the story. This whole situation can't be easy for you."

87

Amber Crewes

Elizabeth seemed to look at Summer for the first time, really taking in who was talking to her. She was clearly touched by the words.

"Thanks. You're right, it has been difficult."

"If I could just talk to you about a few things. Only until your food's ready."

Summer gestured to the booth where Cousin Fern and Aunt Clara sat. She invited Elizabeth to sit with them so she didn't have to stand in the cold.

"Alright. I guess until the food is ready."

Summer slipped back into the booth next to Aunt Clara while Elizabeth set her purse next to Cousin Fern. Unfortunately, it was a victory short-lived as Cousin Fern turned to Elizabeth with an instant accusation.

"How can you be in a relationship with the Mayor when his wife just died? Doesn't that *bother* you?"

Summer's eyes darted to Fern, trying to give a warning glance that would quiet her, but it didn't work. Fern glared at Elizabeth, and the woman immediately grabbed her purse and headed for the door.

"Wait," Summer cried out, chasing her.

If the full diner wasn't watching them before, they certainly were now.

"I'm not answering any questions," Elizabeth insisted. She glared at Summer, as if accusing her of tricking her. "Shelly, I'll be outside."

A Hairy Scary Christmas

"I'm so sorry about that," Summer said as she followed her into the chill winter air. "I never know what's going to come out of her mouth. I promise I didn't know she would say something so awful."

"Leave me alone."

Elizabeth folded her arms across her chest, shivering without a proper winter coat on. Suddenly Aunt Clara was outside too, apologizing.

"I'm so sorry. That woman doesn't know when to keep her mouth closed."

"We know you're innocent in all of this," Summer said, hoping to calm the situation.

This wasn't really the truth—Summer didn't have any proof yet that would clear Elizabeth as a witness—but she needed Elizabeth to trust her again.

"Are you alright, miss?"

The deep voice of Deputy Mason cut across the parking lot as he opened the car door. He strode across the street and was quickly standing beside Elizabeth.

"I'm just here to pick up food," Elizabeth said. "I knew I should have asked for delivery."

Deputy Mason was suddenly staring directly at Summer.

"You shouldn't be here."

"I'm having lunch with my family," she said, struggling to read Mason's expression.

"In the parking lot?"

Amber Crewes

He had them there. Summer froze, unable to come up with a reasonable explanation for why their food was inside while they were out here.

"Why don't you go back to your meal?" he asked. "I'll wait with Miss Elizabeth until her food is ready. You don't need to get involved."

He said these final words with conviction, making Summer think he was speaking about much more than lunch orders. There would be no more talking to Elizabeth now that Deputy Mason was by her side. The only thing Summer and Aunt Clara could do was turn around and push their way back into the diner.

12

"It was a disaster," Summer sighed. "Any hope of being respected by Deputy Mason went right out the window when he saw me chasing a woman out into the parking lot."

"I'm sure it wasn't that bad."

But even as Evan said this, a wide smile spread across his face.

"Don't laugh," she said. "It was *not* my finest moment. But I was trying to repair things after Cousin Fern's outburst."

"You can't win 'em all," he told her as he wrapped colorful lights around the wooden rails of her balcony.

Barney stood just inside the house, watching Evan and Summer on the balcony. The sliding door was open, and Barney barked at them, clearly unhappy with the cold air rushing into the apartment.

"We're almost done, Barney," she said.

Amber Crewes

Her own fingers were frozen. They had purchased far too many lights, so Evan had decided to wrap every bar on the balcony railing. It was a colorful display, and despite the cold air tonight, Summer had to admit it looked good.

"Think it's enough to win the Christmas contest? Maybe I'll be the dark horse."

"Did you *see* your neighbor's house?" Evan asked. "It's a work of art over there."

Summer looked toward the house, where Christmas lights were strung on every corner of the house and around every window. They had candles in the windows and light-up reindeer with heads that moved up and down. Even the path from the driveway to the front door was lined with lights. They had an excellent view of the impressive display from their spot on the balcony.

"Okay, so I'm not winning," she laughed. "But maybe I can try for second place?"

"Hmmm...would you settle for honorable mention?"

"Hey! You're the one who encouraged me to decorate. Don't you have faith in me?"

"Of course I do, but I also know there are a handful of women who start planning their displays in July. Your neighbor is only one of five or six people with displays like that."

Summer connected the final string of lights to the already-lit strands. She handed it to Evan to put the final touches on the balcony.

"I thought you said the contest wasn't a big deal."

A Hairy Scary Christmas

"I said it's not *popular*. But this competition is a *huge* deal for those who participate. Your neighbor here is one of the women who takes things very seriously."

As if on cue, Summer heard the rumble of a garage door, and her neighbor's garage opened. She saw the woman exit the garage carrying something large in her arms. A cord dragged along behind her as she crunched along the frozen grass to the center of her yard. With all the lights on Summer's balcony and in her neighbor's yard, she could see her neighbor clearly.

The woman waved at Summer and Evan on the balcony, and they waved back.

"She has even more decorations," Evan laughed as they watched her spread what looked like a piece of plastic across the yard. It was brown, with elements of red and black.

"What is it?"

They didn't have to wait long to find out. Once the neighbor had the plastic where she wanted it, she found the cord and walked her way to the end of it. She was out of sight for a moment, but Summer felt sure she was finding a spot to plug it in.

With a whirr and a hum, they heard the motor click on, and quickly, the plastic on the ground began to inflate. The decoration rose higher and higher until they were staring at a six-foot-tall reindeer, complete with antlers and a red, blinking nose.

"That's impressive," Evan said. "Nice job, Angela."

"Angela?"

Amber Crewes

The name sparked something in Summer, and she wondered why it sounded familiar.

"That's your neighbor," he said. "Angela Robbins."

All at once, the name clicked. This was the name Mrs. Palmer gave her at the salon. Angela Robbins was Margaret's friend. And she was the one who had, supposedly, found Margaret crying over the Mayor's infidelity.

"Angela Robbins," she repeated. "I think we should go say hello. We can tell her how nice the lights look."

"And ask her about Margaret?" Evan asked, but Summer only smirked.

———

"I'm so glad you like them. If they can bring joy to one person, then I've done my job."

Angela Robbins had a short brown bob tucked under her winter hat. Her cheeks were red from the cold, but she had a warm smile that Summer was quickly drawn to.

"I love looking out my window to see them," Summer assured her. "I don't have much space of my own, so it's nice to have so much Christmas cheer right nearby."

"Oh, but what you've done to your balcony is just darling."

"That's all Evan's doing," she smiled, nudging Evan with her shoulder. "I don't usually decorate, but it seemed like a fitting tribute. I know many people are decorating in honor of Margaret."

A Hairy Scary Christmas

Tears instantly filled Angela's eyes.

"She would be so happy to see what a positive impact she had on the town. I only wish it didn't take her death for it to happen."

"Were you friendly with her?" Evan asked.

Summer watched closely for any signs of guilt or dishonesty, but the woman in front of her seemed genuinely hurt and full of love for her departed friend.

"We were great friends."

Angela looked off, lost in thought. The sound of the whirring motor, as it kept the reindeer inflated, was the only sound they heard for a solid minute.

"When was the last time you saw her?" Summer asked gently.

"It was the night before...the night before they..."

"Found her?"

Angela nodded, looking grateful that she didn't have to say the words. Meanwhile, Summer had to hide her excitement. If Angela had been with Margaret the night before she was found, they may have just confirmed an important piece of her timeline.

"Can you tell me about that? Where were you?"

"It was a meeting for those of us participating in the decorating contest. They're held bi-weekly starting in November. It's a time for the participants to ask questions and receive support from the town council. Though a lot of times they're not so innocent."

95

Amber Crewes

"What do you mean?"

"I've never cared much about medals and accolades, but some of the women in this competition were quite competitive. Some people use the meetings to make complaints about neighbors or accuse them of breaking the rules."

"Are there *rules* for decorating?" Evan asked.

Angela nodded.

"Many of them. But they're hard to enforce. There are easy things, like all decorations need to relate to Christmas or the Christmas season. But then there are rules about putting lights up yourself versus hiring a company. And other rules about the appropriate height for a Santa Claus."

"That sounds intense."

"Yes, it was for some."

"Is that how Margaret saw it?"

She knew Angela didn't want to speak badly of her friend, but Angela's honesty won out, and she nodded.

"Yes, she took it *very* seriously. I often had to remind her it was a silly competition. Otherwise, she would throw her whole life into the contest."

"What time was the meeting?" Summer asked.

"Seven o'clock. We do it after dinner, and everyone brings something for dessert. That meeting ran a bit long. I remember being anxious to leave because I needed to get my kids to bed. I think we wrapped up around eight-thirty."

"And where was it?" Evan asked.

A Hairy Scary Christmas

"The church lets us use the basement. The pastor's wife enjoys the competition, though she doesn't decorate much herself."

Summer blew warm air into her frozen fingers. She knew Angela wouldn't stay out here talking to them for much longer, but she still had so many things she wanted to know.

"How did Margaret seem? The night before she...?"

"She seemed upset. I got there early, and she was crying."

"Do you know why?"

Summer held her breath, wondering if Mrs. Palmer's suspicions would be confirmed. But then Angela shook her head.

"She only said she didn't want to talk about it. She said this Christmas competition was her happy place, and she wanted to forget about everything else for an hour. I just can't believe she's gone."

Angela sniffed, and her eyes filled with tears again. She began to excuse herself, saying she needed some hot chocolate and a good cry. But Summer called out to her.

"One more question. Who knew about the meeting at the church?"

She thought for a moment.

"Anyone on the Decorating Competition email list. It includes anyone who has signed up to be a part of the competition. You don't think someone at the meeting could have done something, do you?"

97

Amber Crewes

"You tell me," Summer said. "You know those women better than I do."

"Of course not. We just gather in a room to gab about decorations and eat too many cookies. No one in that group would harm Margaret."

"Thanks. We'll let you get inside," Summer said.

"Enjoy your hot chocolate," Evan called out. He wrapped his arm around Summer's shoulders, and they waved goodbye to Angela. Then he guided her back into the apartment.

"We're back, Barney," she said to her barking dog. "And we have a new piece of the timeline. A piece of information the police don't have."

13

As Summer approached the salon the next morning, she noticed the lights were already on inside. *Strange. Did Mrs. Beesley get in early?*

She walked a bit faster, telling herself not to panic. It was unusual that she wasn't the first one through the door in the morning, but maybe someone had an early appointment. After all, they were very busy for the holidays.

"Hello?"

She called into the salon as she pushed through the unlocked door.

"Is anyone here?"

No response.

Summer stepped forward, though she wondered if she should step outside and call the police. Margaret's death had her on edge, and she couldn't help wondering if

Amber Crewes

someone was upset with her for looking into things. Her heart pounded as she walked deeper into the salon.

A noise made her freeze. Was someone in the back office?

"Mrs. Beesley, are you here?"

There was another clatter from the back room, and she nearly jumped out of her skin.

"Who's there?"

Suddenly, a head popped out of the office, and Summer recognized the bright red hair Misty had given herself for the holiday season. She let out the breath she had been holding.

"Misty, you nearly gave me a heart attack."

But just as Misty emerged from the office, another person followed her out.

"Deputy Mason. I didn't know you were here."

"Sorry, Summer." Misty's cheeks turned as red as her hair as the couple walked toward her. "Mason has an early shift, and he offered to drop me off at the salon."

"We didn't know someone would be here this early," Mason explained, looking flustered.

Summer held back a smirk at their embarrassment.

"Just be glad I'm not Mrs. Beesley. She would *not* be happy to know you were back there in her office."

"Oh, it wasn't like that," Misty said quickly, her face growing even redder. "I was only in there to drop the mail on her desk. I promise Summer..."

100

A Hairy Scary Christmas

Summer chuckled, crossing to her station to put down her bag.

"It's alright, Misty. Your secret is safe with me."

"I should go," Mason said.

He gave Misty a stiff kiss on the cheek, clearly unsure how to act now that Summer was in the room. Summer felt uncomfortable herself, but not because she had found these two in the salon. No, she was unsure what he thought of her after the incident at the diner yesterday.

"Deputy Mason," she said. "About yesterday…"

"Summer, I can't speak to you about the case."

"No, it's not that. I only wanted to apologize. I wasn't trying to ambush Elizabeth or cause any trouble. Unfortunately, my relatives aren't the most tactful bunch. Misty can tell you that."

"Sure can," Misty nodded with a smile.

"Anyway, my Cousin Fern sometimes talks before she thinks. I was worried she had offended Elizabeth, so I was trying to apologize."

"Hmmm."

Deputy Mason looked at her through narrowed eyes.

"So, you weren't trying to confirm whether Mayor Edwin was in a relationship with his assistant?"

Summer hesitated. As much as she wanted to repair her reputation with the police officer, she knew she couldn't lie. Not if she wanted him to respect her.

Amber Crewes

"Well, I was trying to do that too," she admitted. "But I was *also* trying to apologize for Cousin Fern."

Deputy Mason gave her a rueful smile and a shake of the head.

"Sheriff Brady told me to watch out for you," he chuckled. "I'm starting to think he was right."

"I promise I'm not as bad as Brady makes me out to be."

Deputy Mason glanced at his watch.

"I have to go. I'm going to be late."

Summer remembered her conversation with Angela yesterday. She knew it wasn't right to keep the information to herself. After all, she and the police had the same goal: to find Margaret's killer.

"Wait. Did you know Margaret was at a meeting for the Holiday Decorating Contest the night before she died?"

Mason turned back to her. She saw his eyes go wide and his eyebrows raise.

"Where did you hear that?"

"My neighbor, Angela Robbins. She confirmed it. She was there at the meeting, and she said Margaret was upset. If my information is correct, then it's the last place Margaret was seen alive."

"Good work," he said, impressed. "The Mayor had no idea where Margaret went that night, and her assistant had only written 'meeting' into her planner. If you're right, that's a huge piece of information. Thank you."

A Hairy Scary Christmas

"You're welcome. I just wanted you to know we're on the same side. I want this case solved as much as you do."

"I keep telling him he can trust you," Misty said. "But in case you couldn't tell, he's a pretty cautious guy."

"Alright, I'm out of here. Thanks again, Summer."

Mason gave Misty a final kiss on the cheek and headed for the door. But just as he got there, he turned back, a thoughtful expression on his face.

"Did you forget something?" Misty asked. But Deputy Mason was looking right at Summer.

"You didn't hear it from me," he said. "But the coroner believes she was poisoned."

———

Summer and Misty had to scramble to prepare the salon for their first appointments. As they turned on all the lights, wiped down the chairs, and turned on the Christmas music, Summer couldn't stop thinking about Deputy Mason's words.

Margaret Edwin was poisoned.

She remembered the officer at the crime scene and his comment about foaming at the mouth. It all made sense now.

"Welcome to Summer Cuts," Misty said as the door chimed and her first appointment came in. Misty guided the woman to her station, and soon the room was filled with happy conversation about what she wanted to do with her hair and her holiday plans.

103

Amber Crewes

Since Summer's first appointment wasn't here yet, she took the opportunity to send off a text to Aunt Clara.

'Suspected poison.'

The door chimed, and Summer looked up to greet her appointment. But instead of the new client she was expecting, she was met by the smiling face of Alex.

"Surprise!"

"What are you doing here?"

Summer crossed to her best friend and wrapped her in a hug.

"You've been so busy lately. I figured booking an appointment was the only surefire way to see you."

"Have I really been that hard to reach?" Summer asked as she led Alex to her chair. She felt a pang of guilt that she might have been neglecting her friend.

"Don't worry, I've been a bit preoccupied myself. But I'm dying to hear what's going on with you."

As Alex plopped herself into Summer's chair, she couldn't help noticing an unfamiliar ring on her friend's finger. Usually, that meant a new man in Alex's life.

"If you're here, who's watching Barney and Betty?"

"Well...that's an interesting story."

Summer stared at Alex in the mirror, waiting for an explanation. She didn't like the hesitation in Alex's voice.

"I was going to drop them with Clara, but she had a different idea."

A Hairy Scary Christmas

"Oh no..."

"Yeah. She thought watching the dogs might keep Fern distracted. She said it would keep her out of trouble for a few hours."

Summer groaned at the thought of Cousin Fern being responsible for two animals.

"It's only for a few hours," Alex assured her. "How much trouble can they get into?"

"Clearly, you don't know Cousin Fern."

"Well, it's done now," Alex said, brushing aside Summer's concern with a shrug. "She'll call us if there's a problem. Besides, I need all your attention on me right now. What are we going to do with my hair?"

For the next few minutes, the friends went through new hairstyles and color options. Summer even pulled out some of her favorite magazine clippings that she used as inspiration. They decided on long layers to frame Alex's face and some highlights to bring dimension.

"Perfect," Alex said as she settled back into the chair.

As Summer brushed Alex's hair, it was impossible to miss her friend spinning that mysterious ring around her finger.

"So, is there a reason for this new style?"

Alex shrugged.

"It was time for a change. And with all these Christmas parties, there's no better time for it."

"Right," Summer smirked. "So, there's no new man in your life, then?"

105

Amber Crewes

At the words, Alex instantly stopped rotating the ring on her finger. She put her hands on her knees as if willing herself to stay still. Then she looked at Summer in the mirror and smiled.

That was all the proof Summer needed. Alex definitely had a new boyfriend. She only hoped he would turn out to be a nicer guy than the last ones.

"Well then, we better make sure we make this extra special," Summer told her.

Summer walked Alex to the shampoo sink as the familiar excitement of a new hairstyle washed over her. For the next few hours, she forgot about Margaret Edwin and the question of poison. She simply dedicated herself to helping her best friend feel great about herself for the holidays.

14

"It's even better than I imagined," Alex squealed, looking at herself in the mirror. "It's perfect."

"I'm so glad you like it. Now, will you please go rescue our dogs?"

Summer walked Alex to the front and gave her another hug as Alex thanked her profusely. When she sifted through her purse to pay, Summer shook her head.

"No charge for my best friend," she smiled. "You save me hundreds in dog walker fees when you watch Barney, so let's call it even."

"At least let me give you a tip," Alex insisted as she looked through the bills in her wallet.

"Definitely not. You do too much for me already."

"But I can't give you nothing!"

An idea popped into Summer's head, and she looked squarely at her friend, a challenge on her face.

107

Amber Crewes

"Alright, here's what you can do: tell me about this new boyfriend of yours."

Alex scoffed, clearly surprised by the request. Summer felt a surge of satisfaction, knowing Alex had walked herself right into that trap. But just when she thought she would finally get some information, Alex turned away from her with a smirk. She waltzed over to the coat rack to pull her coat down and then whirled it dramatically around her shoulders.

"We'll have lots of time for that," she said. "If I tell you about it now, what will we talk about at Christmas dinner?"

Summer groaned.

"You know I don't like unsolved mysteries. Couldn't you give me a *hint*?"

But Alex only shook her head.

"Sorry. Right now, I need to go rescue our dogs from your cousin, remember?" she teased, turning Summer's own words against her.

"Fine," Summer sighed. "But that means I get all the dirt at Christmas. A full debriefing on who he is, how you met, and how things are going."

"Deal."

Alex lifted her hat to her head, but she paused.

"Nope, I can't do it. I'd rather have cold ears than mess up this beautiful new hair. Thanks again, Summer. It really is beautiful."

A Hairy Scary Christmas

With that, Alex spun out of the salon, pushing her way through the door just as Summer's phone chimed. She looked down to a text from Aunt Clara.

'Poison? And her last known location was the Christmas meeting. We need to find out who was there.'

'You think someone at the meeting poisoned her?' Summer texted back. She couldn't imagine someone like the sweet Angela Robbins setting out to hurt Margaret. But Summer knew it wasn't fair to assume everyone at the meeting was as kind and soft-spoken as her neighbor.

'We can't rule it out.'

Summer stared at the phone. For so long, her list of suspects had been tiny, barely anyone except for Mayor Edwin. But it would quickly become a very long list if they added everyone who attended the Holiday Decorating Meeting.

As Summer composed a response, Mrs. Beesley burst through the door, surprising her. She hadn't scheduled herself for any appointments this morning, so Summer wasn't expecting her until this afternoon.

"I knew it," she cried, instantly angry. Summer wondered if she had done something to make Mrs. B upset. She wracked her brain, but she couldn't remember doing anything wrong today.

"Is everything alright?"

Mrs. Beesley reached around the reception desk to grab the television remote. She pushed the power button, and the TV buzzed to life, showing the news.

"I knew Ellen Avery had something to do with this."

Amber Crewes

Summer recognized the woman from the political commercial Evan had shown her at dinner. Ellen Avery was now on the news, speaking directly to the camera in a clip of what was coming up.

"I'm here today because I have information on Margaret Edwin's death. Information that I can no longer keep silent, no matter how many people want me to."

"Oh my." Misty was suddenly next to them, along with her client, who looked equally as intrigued. The woman had foil all over her head as her color set, but her eyes were glued to the screen. All four of them were transfixed by the television and Ellen Avery's promise of information. A reporter came onto the screen and announced,

"When we return, Ellen Avery tells us what she knows. After a brief word from our sponsors."

The reporter sent them to a commercial, and an advertisement for laundry detergent began to play.

"She has information?" Summer asked. "What do you think that means?"

"It means she's doing whatever it takes to get elected," Mrs. Beesley said dismissively.

"I'll bet she doesn't have anything," Misty's client said. "It's just a way for the news to get more ratings. Whatever they can do to keep us all glued to the screen, right?"

"Looks like it's working," Misty snorted.

"Her past political ads made reference to a 'secret'," Summer mused. "Is she finally going to tell everyone what that means?"

A Hairy Scary Christmas

"I guess we're about to find out," Misty said.

———

"I have proof that Mayor Stewart Edwin was having an affair with his assistant, Ms. Elizabeth Jenkins. Multiple people within the mayor's office have confirmed this report."

Summer was shocked, not by the information, since she already knew it. Instead, she was shocked that Ellen Avery could make such a blatant accusation on live television. Had the news vetted her story? If she had proof, where was it?

"Can she just say something like that?" Misty asked, echoing Summer's thoughts. "It doesn't seem right."

"It's sensational," Mrs. Beesley said. "All orchestrated to get her more votes."

Ellen Avery continued speaking to the news reporter, who was interviewing her.

"I've turned in incriminating evidence to the Spring Harbor police department. They are reviewing the evidence, which is why I cannot give you the details at this time."

"How convenient," Misty's client said under her breath.

Summer had to agree with her. It was easy for someone to say they had proof, but much harder for someone to actually present it. She was starting to agree with Mrs. Beesley that Ellen Avery was simply trying to cause a sensation to get herself more votes.

"Come on." Misty touched her client on the shoulder and

Amber Crewes

guided her back to the chair. "Let's get this color washed out."

Summer and Mrs. Beesley stayed by the reception desk as the reporter asked Ellen Avery what this affair had to do with Margaret's death.

"You must remember that I'm only coming forward for Margaret's sake," Ellen Avery announced. Summer rolled her eyes as the woman pulled a handkerchief from her pocket and dabbed her eyes. The reporter encouraged her to continue.

"After what I have learned about this affair and recent events, it's clear to me that Margaret Edwin found out about her husband's affair. I even have a witness who says Margaret was crying about her husband's infidelity the night before she was found dead."

Mrs. Beesley gasped, but Summer remembered her chatty client from yesterday.

"I hope she checked that out," she said. "I had a client tell me the same thing yesterday, but when I went to the original source, she said Margaret didn't tell her why she was crying."

"And why is that significant?" The news reporter asked, clearly guiding Ellen toward even more scandalous accusations.

"If Margaret Edwin was crying about her husband the night before her death, then we can only conclude one thing."

She paused for dramatic effect. It was just long enough for Summer to feel sick to her stomach as she began to see where Ellen was leading the conversation.

112

A Hairy Scary Christmas

"It's clear that Margaret found out about the affair and then took her own life to escape the embarrassment and shame of the situation."

"What?" Mrs. Beesley cried. "She would never do that."

"Now she's just making things up," Summer said, shaking her head. "The police have already determined this to be a suspicious death. She's going against the facts of the case."

"I know this information is shocking," Ellen told the viewers. "It has taken me time to process it myself, but it is the only logical conclusion I can come to. I know it is difficult to realize that people you like and love have shortcomings. We all expect our mayor to be honest and trustworthy. It's shocking to realize he has been sneaking around behind his wife's back and lying to this town for years. That is why it's time for someone else to run this town. And it's why I'm running for mayor in this upcoming election."

"Of course, it's all a political stunt," Summer said. "You were right."

"This is too much. Attacking your political opponent is one thing, but now she's dragging Margaret into it. Now the whole town will think she killed herself?"

"Not the whole town," Summer assured her. "And definitely not the people working this case. Don't worry, Mrs. Beesley. The police and I know this was no suicide, and it was no accident. Margaret Edwin was murdered, and we're going to do everything we can to find out who is responsible."

15

"Do you think she's doing it to get elected?" Aunt Clara asked.

Summer sat across from Aunt Clara and Carl in the cafe, waiting for their afternoon coffee orders to arrive. She was pleased to see how busy the cafe was today. Nearly every table was filled with people with shopping bags at their feet as they took a break from Christmas shopping.

"That's definitely why she's going on the news to drag the Mayor through the mud," Carl agreed.

"Right. But I'm saying...what if she did more than just spread rumors? What if she was responsible for Margaret's death?"

Summer dropped her voice as she said it, since she didn't need the whole cafe to hear her accusing Ellen Avery of murder. But the idea had been bouncing around in her head all afternoon.

Amber Crewes

"You think she was so desperate to win that she resorted to murder?"

Summer shrugged.

"Do you think I'm crazy?"

"Of course you are," Evan said as he appeared at the table to deposit their coffees. He smiled at Summer to show her he was only joking and then asked what they were talking about.

"Summer's accusing people of murder," Aunt Clara explained.

"That sounds about right."

Carl pulled his wallet from his pocket and handed over his credit card.

"This round's on me," he told Evan. Evan thanked him and went to the register to run his card. Summer watched Aunt Clara look sideways at him and suddenly a gloom descended over the table.

"Well now."

She grunted, clearly wanting Carl to sense her displeasure. Summer sat still, uncomfortable to be in the middle of whatever tension was brewing between them.

"What is it?" Carl asked.

"I just find it interesting that you're being so generous with your money."

Carl rolled his eyes and sighed.

"This is about the motorcycle, isn't it?"

A Hairy Scary Christmas

"You can go around buying coffee for everyone willy-nilly, but when I ask you for a Christmas present, you tell me it's extravagant. And that's after I made sure you did well in Cousin Fern's little game."

"Aunt Clara, don't say that too loud," Summer scolded. "We don't need people to know you were involved in that."

"I think I'll leave you girls to talk," Carl said. He stood up from the table and lifted his full coffee mug. "I'm sure Evan can put this in a to-go cup."

Summer thought Aunt Clara would encourage him to stay, but she didn't even look at him. Instead, she used her finger to lift a dollop of whipped cream to her mouth.

"What was that?" Summer asked as Carl left them. "Are you really upset with him because he won't buy you that motorcycle?"

"Of course not," she said as she popped her finger into her mouth. "But if I don't keep reminding him, how will I know he'll follow through? I'm bound and determined to see that motorcycle in my driveway on Christmas morning."

She shook her head at her aunt, laughing over the lengths she would go to get her way. But Summer knew her aunt well. The behavior shouldn't be a surprise.

"Now, let's get back to Ellen Avery," Clara coaxed. "Why would she have to kill Margaret? Wouldn't the information about the affair be enough?"

"I don't think so. After all, she tried that last time. In her ad campaign, she kept alluding to a 'secret', which had to be the affair. But even when most of the town knew what she was referring to, Mayor Edwin was re-elected."

Amber Crewes

"So, she needed something bigger."

Summer nodded as Aunt Clara put the pieces together. It was a theory that was starting to sound more and more plausible the more they talked about it.

"Her behavior seems to be getting more and more desperate," Summer said. "How else do you describe her little news conference today? I don't think we can rule her out."

"No, we can't. Just like we can't rule out the people at that Decorating Contest meeting. We need to find out who was there."

Summer had been thinking of this ever since Aunt Clara's text earlier today. But she didn't know how they could find out who was there without asking every person in town. Or driving around to see who had Christmas lights up.

"I could ask my neighbor, Angela, but it could make her suspicious. She might warn some of them that we're asking around about them.

"Isn't the contest sponsored by the Town Council?" Clara asked. "Surely they will have a list? They need to judge the houses, after all."

"That's brilliant," Summer agreed.

"Good. Let's go see."

Aunt Clara stood up, sloshing hot chocolate onto the table as she lifted her mug.

"Now?" Summer asked, but Clara was already heading for the door, taking Evan's ceramic mug with her.

A Hairy Scary Christmas

"Hi there. We're looking for the list of participants for the Holiday Decorating Contest."

Summer and Aunt Clara stood in front of the desk of a petite woman wearing thick-rimmed glasses, her hair pulled tight into a ponytail. She stared at them blankly, making Summer wonder if she had heard anything they said.

"The Holiday Decorating Contest," Aunt Clara echoed. "Councilman Elias is the chair of that committee, is he not?"

Summer and Aunt Clara had already been on a wild goose chase through City Hall. Simply finding the person organizing the contest had been a scavenger hunt in and of itself. They had finally been given the name of Councilman Elias and his office number.

"He is."

"Good. Then could you give us a list of participants?"

Summer held her face in a smile despite her frustration at this woman of few words.

"I could, but I will not."

She heard Aunt Clara sigh, and grabbed her wrist before she could say anything negative. She worried Aunt Clara was about to destroy any chance they had of getting the list of names they needed to begin chipping away at their suspects.

"We...well, I," Summer stuttered. "I'm working with the police to help investigate the Margaret Edwin case. And we

119

Amber Crewes

know she was involved in the contest. It's simply a formality —we need to check on those who were with her that evening."

"You're working with the police?" the woman asked. Summer nodded, reasoning that this wasn't too much of a stretch. If her exchange of information with Deputy Mason this morning wasn't cooperation, what was it?

"I am. Deputy Mason and I are investigating."

She ignored Aunt Clara's questioning look and kept her eyes on the woman whose nameplate read 'Cecile Bullar'.

"If that's true, then why did the police come by here earlier today to get the same information?"

She froze. She hadn't expected the police to follow up so quickly on her tip. Now she had all but revealed her lie to Cecile, who was already hesitant to help them.

"They asked us to get a second copy," Aunt Clara chimed in, making Summer inwardly groan. It made them sound even more ridiculous. Cecile blinked at them.

"They don't have a copy machine at the police station?"

Summer waited to see how Aunt Clara would respond to this, but her aunt chose that moment to be silent. The woman always had something to say, but right now, she simply looked at Summer.

"Right," she said. "That's a good thought. Well..."

"Summer?"

The voice of someone behind her was a welcome distraction, and Summer turned to see Deputy Mason

A Hairy Scary Christmas

walking down the hallway. He stepped into the council member's office to greet them.

"Deputy Mason," Summer smiled. "It's good to see you."

"You too," he said. He looked between Summer and Cecile, who was still scowling behind the desk.

"Is everything alright?" he asked.

All at once, Cecile jumped to her feet. She bent over her computer and began typing and clicking.

"Of course," Cecile said. "I was just helping with your request. It will only take a moment."

A flash of confusion crossed Deputy Mason's face, but he said nothing. He had to know why Summer was here. After all, he had come to this very office earlier in the day for the same thing. But thankfully, he said nothing.

"Here's the list, Deputy Mason."

Cecile handed the printed pages across the desk as she flashed a smile at Deputy Mason.

"Thanks so much," Summer said. "We really appreciate it."

"Anything to help the police," Cecile said, clearly flirting with the handsome deputy.

They thanked her, and Summer and Aunt Clara left the office and crossed into the hall with Deputy Mason on their heels.

"You're helping the police, are you?" he asked.

Summer shrugged, feigning innocence.

121

Amber Crewes

"I only mentioned we were friends," she explained. "I guess she got confused."

"Hmm."

Deputy Mason looked carefully at her as if he wanted to say more. But instead, he gave her a half-smile.

"Friends," he muttered, and then he turned and walked away, leaving Summer with a fresh list of suspects in her hand.

16

"Misty's going to take my afternoon appointment. It should give us some time to go through this list." Summer and Aunt Clara piled back into Summer's car, welcoming the heater's warmth.

"Back to the cafe?" Summer asked.

"Let's look over it at the Manor House Inn. We can kill two birds with one stone while I check in on Fern."

"You got it," Summer said, heading for the inn. "But tell me what I'm walking in to here. Is Cousin Fern going to be happy to see us?"

Aunt Clara shrugged.

"Your guess is as good as mine. But as long as she's not getting into trouble, I don't care if she bites my head off."

"Do you think I made things worse with Deputy Mason?"

She couldn't figure out whether the interaction had been a positive one. On one hand, he didn't send them away or take

Amber Crewes

away the list of names. But he had also caught Summer in a lie.

"We got what we came for, didn't we?" Aunt Clara said. "I'd say the ends justify the means. That's my motto lately, anyway."

Summer had a feeling she knew what Aunt Clara was talking about.

"As long as that motorcycle shows up in your driveway, you don't care what it takes to get it there?"

"Precisely."

Summer shook her head as she pulled into a parking spot at the Manor House. She wanted to point out to Aunt Clara just how similar she was to Fern, but she feared it would only make Clara grumpy.

"I had a feeling I'd see you two today."

Cousin Fern was in the sitting room to the left of the entrance. It was a cozy room with a fireplace and an old piano that was long out of tune. Fern had a notebook in front of her, writing something.

"We're happy to see you looking so peaceful," Summer said. "Care to help us with the case?"

Cousin Fern's eyes lit up even as Aunt Clara gave her a warning look. But if they were going to sit here looking over this list, they might as well let Fern help. Wasn't Aunt Clara always looking for ways to keep her occupied?

"What's on the docket?" Fern asked. She put her notebook down, and the three of them moved to a small table in the corner.

124

A Hairy Scary Christmas

"We believe Margaret's last known location was at a meeting for the Holiday Decorating Contest. That's the last place anyone saw her before she was found in her car behind the craft store."

Summer laid the list out in front of them. It was two and a half printed pages, perhaps twenty-five or thirty names.

"I didn't think so many people participated," Clara mused. "Margaret was practically the only one who ever won."

"Are you sure everyone here is participating?" Fern asked. "It could be anyone who signed up for information."

They scanned the names, hoping that something would jump out at them.

"There," Summer said, dropping her finger onto the second page. "Ellen Avery."

Aunt Clara shook her head.

"Now I *know* she doesn't have Christmas lights up. She lives around the corner from me, and her house is the darkest one on the block."

"Then I was right," Fern said. "It's an interest list. These are the people who signed up for the emails."

Summer's head spun at the implications.

"Then even people who aren't participating could have found out about the meeting. Do you think Ellen Avery signed up so she could track Margaret's movements?"

"What about the Mayor's assistant?" Clara asked. "Is Elizabeth on here?"

Amber Crewes

They checked the list multiple times, but they didn't find an Elizabeth, Liz, or Lizzie.

"We should sign up. If there's another meeting, then we need to be there."

The reception desk for the Manor House Inn was right in the entryway. It was currently unoccupied, and Summer rushed over to click her way to the internet.

"And you think *I'm* trouble?" Fern asked under her breath.

"I'll only use it for a second," Summer said. She typed in the town hall website and clicked her way to the information page about the decorating contest. There, at the bottom, was a button to sign up for the email list. Summer added her information and double-checked her email address, then she hit 'Submit'.

"Click out of it so he doesn't know you were on there. And erase the history."

Summer didn't want to know how Fern knew to do those things, but she did as she said. She clicked out of the browser, revealing an email open on the screen. She wasn't trying to pry, but the subject of the email caught her attention.

"Um, Aunt Clara?"

"What is it?"

Clara crossed to the computer with Fern trailing behind her. The three of them looked at an email from Ellen Avery's campaign. There was a rally tonight, and she was calling her supporters to attend.

126

A Hairy Scary Christmas

'Come to the Mayor's Office', the email said. *'It's time to make the man account for what he's done.'*

As Summer, Aunt Clara, and Cousin Fern piled into her car, Summer checked her phone. She had a message from Evan asking if she wanted to go to dinner.

'Can't,' she texted back. *'I have to go to a political rally.'*

Summer glanced at the clock, which read 5:23. The rally had started at 5:15, so they were going to be a few minutes late. Thankfully, they were only a few minutes away.

"Remember, Cousin Fern, no outbursts. We can't have a repeat of what happened at the diner."

"Oh, enough with you. I know how to handle myself."

"I'm texting Carl for some backup," Clara noted from the passenger seat. If anything goes wrong at this rally, it will be good to have a former police officer there."

"Good thinking. But let's hope it's not needed."

As they pulled into the small parking lot of city hall, they saw a group of about twenty people lined up at the bottom of the stone steps. Many held signs, and they could tell they were chanting something even before they opened the car doors.

"What do we want?"

"The Truth!"

"When do we want it?"

127

Amber Crewes

"Now!"

Ellen Avery was at the top of the steps, urging the crowd on with a megaphone. She paced back and forth at the top of the steps, looking down at her followers.

"Not too many of them," Cousin Fern commented, but Summer shushed her as they approached the crowd.

"Excuse me," Summer said to a woman holding a sign over her head. "Could you tell me what's going on?"

Summer often found it was a good idea to pretend you didn't know anything about these events. It gave her information on why people were there, and what they thought the purpose was.

"We're here to *demand* that Mayor Edwin admit to his affair. It's the only way to get justice for Margaret."

"Is that why you're here?" Clara asked. "Because you care about Margaret? Or are you supporting Ellen Avery?"

"Isn't it the same thing? We can't have a mayor who is so dishonest."

Ellen began another chant, urging the crowd to be louder. She insisted they only needed to scream loud enough, and the Mayor would come out. Summer scanned the crowd, trying to clock any recognizable faces. It was then that they heard the wail of the police car.

The Sheriff peeled into the parking lot and Summer groaned, knowing Brady wouldn't be happy to see her. A flash momentarily blinded her as someone took photos of the crowd.

A Hairy Scary Christmas

"We're not doing anything wrong," Ellen called to the crowd, many of whom were recognizably nervous.

The voice of Sheriff Brady echoed through the speaker of the cop car.

"Alright, everyone, it's time to wrap this up. Go home."

Brady stepped out of the car and walked toward the steps as Ellen Avery raced down them.

"You can't send us home," she announced, standing on her toes so she was face-to-face with the sheriff. "We have a right to protest."

"Not when you're blocking the entrance," Brady explained. "People are afraid to come in and out."

"That's the point," Ellen told him, but already members of the crowd were starting to disperse. Ellen tried to encourage them, telling them they only needed to wait a little longer so they could face the Mayor as they intended. But it didn't work.

"That's right, everyone," Brady said. "Just head on home and have your dinner."

As he scanned the crowd, he locked eyes with Summer. He didn't try to hide the scowl on his face.

"Let's get out of here," Summer said. "This was a waste of time."

"What did I miss?" Carl arrived just in time to see everyone leaving.

"Nothing," Aunt Clara mumbled. "A whole lot of nothing."

Amber Crewes

"Good," Carl said. "The last thing we need is for anyone to get hurt."

Carl and Aunt Clara offered to drive Cousin Fern back to the Inn.

"Thanks," Summer said. "Maybe I can still catch Evan for some dinner."

They said their goodbyes and headed to their cars, but Summer could still hear Clara complaining to Carl.

"You know what would have gotten you here faster?" Clara asked. "A motorcycle."

17

When Summer woke up the following day, she found a mysterious text from Mrs. Beesley.

'Misty and I can handle things today. No need to come in.'

Everything about this seemed strange. Summer knew how busy the salon was these days because she had checked the appointments herself. And why was Mrs. Beesley telling her whether to come into her own salon? Of course, Summer would go in today.

But then she realized the gift Mrs. Beesley might be giving her. Christmas dinner was fast approaching, and Summer hadn't done any grocery shopping. She had invited all these people over, and she was about to have no food for them. She decided she could use the morning to grocery shop and then swing by the salon for some afternoon appointments. She texted Aunt Clara as she sipped her coffee.

'Send me your grocery list. I'm going shopping.'

Amber Crewes

She was pleased when she immediately responded with a long list of ingredients. Using Aunt Clara's list and her own preferences, she put together the shopping list.

'Want to play hooky and go grocery shopping with me?'

She knew Evan was busy at the cafe, but he had some solid employees who could handle things without him for a few hours. She was pleased when he texted that he would pick her up in ten minutes.

When they arrived at the store, the parking lot was filled with cars coming in and out.

"It's busy," she noted. "For some reason, I thought it wouldn't be so bad on a weekday."

"Christmas is in two days," Evan laughed. "What did you expect?"

They weaved their way up and down the aisles, reaching around people and dodging shopping carts. As Summer walked, she couldn't help feeling that people were a bit too interested in her today. Several shoppers seemed to be staring at her. A few even frowned in her direction.

"Isn't it supposed to be Christmas?" she asked as they shivered in the frozen food aisle. "Why is everyone so grumpy?"

"Don't worry about it," Evan said, dropping frozen peas into the basket. "They'll get over it soon enough."

"Aunt Clara needs Cream of Mushroom soup. Did we already pass that aisle?"

They retraced their steps to find the aisle with all the canned soups. Summer was shocked by the number of

132

A Hairy Scary Christmas

options. Finding the mushroom among the Cream of Celery and Cream of Chicken seemed to take forever.

"How dare you?"

The voice was loud and aggressive, right next to Summer's ear. She blinked and looked up, shocked to find the woman was staring right at her.

"Excuse me?" she asked. But the woman snatched a can from the shelf and pushed her cart away aggressively.

"What is going on today?" she asked. Evan looked a bit confused.

"Do you really not know?"

"What are you talking about?"

Instead of answering, he took hold of the cart and pushed it toward the check-out. Summer had no choice but to follow.

"There. You didn't see it?"

He pointed to the day's newspaper, which had the salacious title "Protesters Impede Justice". And just below the headline, in a color photo that nearly crossed the full page, was a photo of Summer at the bottom of the steps, the full crowd gathered behind her. It almost looked like Summer had organized the protest instead of Ellen Avery. Ellen was only a small figure in the background of the photo.

"This isn't fair," she said. "I wasn't even there to protest."

"It'll blow over," Evan shrugged. "They just need something to sell papers."

"This is why everyone's mad at me," she realized. "They

133

Amber Crewes

think I was causing problems at city hall. They probably think I'm part of Ellen Avery's conspiracy theories."

"Let's get out of here." Evan placed a hand on Summer's back to guide her to the nearest cashier. Despite his support, she couldn't help feeling discouraged.

"I'm trying to help," she said to no one in particular. "I want to figure out what happened to Margaret, just like everyone else. Why does it feel like I'm only making things worse?"

———

They made it to the parking lot without any further verbal altercations, though there were more sneers and glares in Summer's direction. She finally understood why Mrs. Beesley had told her she could stay home. She was trying to protect Summer from the wrath of the town this morning.

"Excuse me. Hey, excuse me."

A woman came rushing toward Summer as they loaded the last items into her trunk.

"I wasn't actually participating in the rally," Summer said, trying to intercept this woman's anger. Maybe if she could just explain...

"You can't sign up."

Summer blinked, confused by the words. She looked closer at the woman and realized she recognized her.

"You're Mrs. Cole, right? We met you in the hardware store."

A Hairy Scary Christmas

"You can't sign up," she repeated. Summer looked at Evan. Did he have any idea what she was talking about? But he only gave her a discreet shrug of the shoulders.

"I'm sorry, I don't understand. Is this about the newspaper article?"

"It's about the decorating contest," Wanda Cole said, frustration evident in her voice. "It's too late to sign up."

"Oh, I see."

Summer remembered adding her name to the email list at the Manor House yesterday.

"The deadline was December 15ᵗʰ, and we're well past that. So, you won't be able to participate."

"Right. Well, I actually live in an apartment, so there's no way my lights could compare to someone who owns a full house."

"It doesn't matter. You're not participating."

Wanda Cole scowled at her, looking angrier than any of the people in the store today. What was going on here? Why did everyone in Spring Harbor suddenly hate her?

"How did you know I signed up?" she asked. "I thought Councilman Elias was the chair of that committee."

"I saw your email added to the distribution list. I'm familiar with all the names on that email list—I know who participates. You can't just swoop in at the last minute and try to win everything."

It seemed Wanda Cole had some detective skills of her own. She had seen Summer's email address and instantly

135

connected that it was a new name to the group. Was it strange for this woman to obsess over email lists in that way? Or was it normal behavior for a woman who had nothing to live for except this competition?

"I've never asked," Summer said. "Is there a prize for the winner?"

"Of course, there's a prize. A trophy that gets to sit in the winner's house for the full year. Plus, bragging rights, of course."

"A trophy?" Evan asked. "That's it?"

"If you don't understand, then it's even more reason why you should not participate. This is a town tradition. We only want people involved who will take it seriously."

Wanda Cole turned on her heel and stormed away. She slammed the door of her car and took off.

"I don't think she got any groceries," Evan noted. "She came here just to yell at you."

"Way to rub it in," Summer mumbled.

"If Wanda saw your name on the email distribution list, does that mean you got an email from the committee?"

She was instantly excited, surprised she hadn't thought of that herself. Did the committee send more information on the contest? Or, even better, were they messaging about a new meeting?

Summer found her phone in her jacket pocket and quickly scrolled through the many junk emails.

"Here. I found it."

A Hairy Scary Christmas

She scanned it quickly as Evan read over her shoulder.

"They're judging the houses tonight. And they're going to announce a winner."

"Where?" Evan asked.

"In the church basement. There's a party for all the participants. Then, the judges will come back there to announce the winner."

"And the food?" Evan asked. "If there's a catering company, maybe we can find out how Margaret was poisoned."

"No catering company," Summer said with a shake of her head. "It's a potluck."

18

Evan drove home from the grocery store so Summer could call Aunt Clara.

"There's a meeting tonight," she told her. "It's a perfect chance to see who shows up and maybe ask people about Margaret."

"I guess we're going to church tonight," Clara chuckled. "Now, tell me again about Wanda Cole."

Summer recounted their strange interaction with Wanda. She wondered aloud to Aunt Clara about her suspicions of the woman.

"Maybe she just really cares about Christmas decorations," she suggested. But Aunt Clara had a more sinister take.

"Maybe she cares enough to kill for them."

They pulled up to Summer's apartment, and Evan turned off the car while Summer wrapped up her phone call.

Amber Crewes

"Aunt Clara, I have to get these groceries in the house before anything melts. But I'll see you for the meeting?"

"I'll be there."

Summer hung up and crossed to the trunk, where she began lifting heavy bags into her arms alongside Evan. She was trying to do the mental calculations about whether they would need two trips or if they could carry them all up in one.

"Summer!"

She turned around to see Angela, her neighbor, waving at her over the fence. She was pleased to see the woman was smiling at her, which was certainly a welcome change from her previous interactions this morning.

"Hey, Angela."

"I wanted to thank you."

From their positions across the parking lot, Summer couldn't hear everything Angela was saying. She set the groceries back into the trunk, and Evan did the same. Then they both walked over to her.

"Sorry, I couldn't hear you. What were you saying?"

"I wanted to thank you. I know Ellen can be a polarizing figure these days, but she's a really good person. It's nice to know you're supporting her. Ultimately, it's what Margaret would have wanted, don't you think?"

There was so much information in this small speech that Summer didn't even know where to start. She glanced at Evan, who looked similarly speechless.

140

A Hairy Scary Christmas

"You're talking about the photo?" Summer asked.

"Exactly. I know people think Ellen's doing this all as a stunt or to get more votes. But she truly cares about the moral center of this town. How can we have a mayor who does something like this to his wife?"

"Then you're voting for Ellen?" Evan asked.

"Oh, of course," Angela nodded. "She's my sister-in-law, after all. I think my family might disown me if I didn't."

The woman laughed on the other side of the fence, but Summer was doing anything but laughing. She felt her stomach drop at the words. Angela and Ellen were *family*? Why didn't she know about this?

"I didn't realize you were so close," she said carefully. "It seems like it might be a difficult election. Mayor Edwin is a popular guy."

"It's outrageous," Angela burst out. "His wife died under suspicious circumstances. Can't people see this is all related? He had to be involved in this."

"You think so?" Summer asked. "Last time we spoke, you didn't seem so sure."

"Well, I didn't know you were on Ellen's side. Of course, I have to be careful about who I say things to. This town is getting more and more divisive over this. But we're happy to have you as an ally."

She cringed at the word, but Summer knew now wasn't the time to protest. She had to play along, at least until she could wrap her head around this new information.

141

Amber Crewes

"I saw they're judging the houses tonight," Summer said, nodding toward Angela's decked-out display. It looked like there were even more decorations up since the last time she looked.

"Ooh, are you coming to the party?"

"I'll be there," Summer smiled. "But now I have to get my groceries inside. Good talking to you."

"Bye now."

Angela waved enthusiastically, but Summer kept her head down and made a beeline for the car. She looked at Evan with wide eyes, though they didn't speak until they were in the entryway of her apartment.

"Did you hear that? Angela is Ellen Avery's sister-in-law."

"And she seems very invested in Ellen winning this election," Evan said.

"Angela had more access to Margaret than anyone. She could have easily slipped a cookie onto Margaret's plate or encouraged her to eat a piece of pie she had contaminated."

Summer took a deep breath, shocked by how quickly her theories on this case could change.

"I think we have a new suspect."

———

There were still hours before the Decorating Contest party, and Summer needed to keep herself busy. Evan also needed to get back to the cafe. They drove back downtown and said their goodbyes, planning to meet up again after work.

142

A Hairy Scary Christmas

'Could you keep Barney late tonight?' Summer texted Alex. She wasn't sure how long the contest and the party would last, and she didn't want Barney sitting alone at home.

'Sure thing. It will give me more time for the Christmas photo shoot.'

Alex sent back a picture of Barney and Betty sitting in front of Alex's fireplace. They had bright green sweaters on and reindeer ears. Summer laughed, pleased that Barney was such a good sport with getting dressed up.

"Mrs. Beesley said you weren't coming in today," Misty said as Summer pushed through the door. She glanced at the salon to see it was empty except for Misty and Deputy Mason, eating lunch.

"I appreciate her trying to protect me, but I'm not going to let the town scare me away from my own salon."

"Good for you," Deputy Mason said with a nod. Summer was glad to see him. She had so much new information about the case, and she needed to talk through it.

"I'm glad you're here." Summer crossed to the small table they often pulled out for lunch and took a seat. "My head is swimming with information."

"If you're going to ask me about the case, you can stop right there."

He put his hands up, fending off her conversation, but Summer wouldn't let him stop her. Not when she felt so close to figuring this all out.

"You don't have to tell me anything. But I'm going to talk."

143

Amber Crewes

She thought Mason might protest, but Misty spoke up before he could.

"You really can trust her," she said. "I know Summer well, and she's a good person. Maybe she gets a little too involved sometimes, but it's always for a good reason."

Summer smiled in appreciation. Deputy Mason glanced at Misty, weighing her words. Then he glanced at Summer and gave the briefest of nods. It was all she needed, and words began to pour out of her.

"There's a meeting tonight. The results of the Decorating Contest are going to be announced in the church basement. There's a party for all the participants that will start at 6pm. It's our best chance to scope out the people. Maybe ask some questions about who knows Margaret. Plus, it's a potluck!"

"Do you really think whoever poisoned Margaret would try it again? They poisoned someone once—isn't that enough?"

"I don't know," Summer admitted. "But maybe the coroner can tell us what was inside her stomach. If the same food's at the party, maybe we can narrow in on our killer."

"Only if they bring the same food."

Deputy Mason seemed skeptical, but Summer knew there was something to her theory. Every road was pointing her toward this Christmas party and the people involved in this contest.

"Also, Ellen Avery signed herself up for the contest."

"We know," he nodded. "We have the same email list as you, remember?"

A Hairy Scary Christmas

"Right. But did you know Angela Robbins is Ellen's sister-in-law? And Angela has competed in the contest for years. Apparently, she's one of the few people who has ever beaten Margaret."

She could tell this was new information for the Deputy.

"We spoke to Angela Robbins. It sounded like she was good friends with Margaret. But she never told us about her connection to Ellen Avery."

"You think Ellen Avery poisoned Margaret so she could win the election?" Misty asked.

"Either that, or she had Angela Robbins do it. I think we need to find out if there was anything in Margaret's stomach. It might be the key we need."

There was a pause, and Deputy Mason looked thoughtful. Then he let out a sigh.

"There was food there," he admitted. "Some of it still undigested, so the poison had to be pretty fast acting."

"So, it's likely she ingested it," Summer cried. "Were they able to identify the food?"

Once again, he hesitated before answering.

"They were. It was fruitcake."

19

Summer could barely get through her afternoon appointment. The only thing she could think of was the meeting tonight. Misty offered to close up, so Summer jumped into her car and texted Aunt Clara to say she was on her way.

'I'm at Manor House. Meet me there.'

When she entered the Inn, she was hit with angry voices. Aunt Clara and Fern were arguing.

"I'm not sure why it's any of your business," Cousin Fern said.

She sat in an oversized armchair, her arms across her chest. Aunt Clara stood next to her, holding a notebook in her hand. Summer recognized it as the book Fern was writing in yesterday.

"What's going on?" She asked, stepping into the sitting room.

Amber Crewes

"Your Aunt wants to control my life," Cousin Fern announced.

"I'm only trying to make sure you keep your housing. If you get kicked out of here, where are you going to live?"

"Maybe you can rent me an apartment with that motorcycle money."

"That's enough," Summer said. "Let's keep our voices down."

"Look." Aunt Clara thrust the notebook into Summer's hands. She looked at the pages, seeing a list of names with dollar signs and numbers next to them.

"What is it?"

"Just a game," Fern insisted, but Aunt Clara shook her head.

"She's been taking bets. All of those people gave her money."

"What are they betting on?"

It seemed Aunt Clara hadn't gotten that bit of information out of Cousin Fern. They both looked at her, waiting. Cousin Fern kept her mouth firmly closed, looking smug. But it only took a moment before she sighed and gave in.

"It's for the Holiday Decorating Contest," she said. "I'm taking bets on who's going to win."

"Cousin Fern!" Summer cried. Now she was the one being loud. She adjusted her voice, dropping it lower. "One of those people might have *killed* Margaret Edwin. And now you're making bets on their houses?"

A Hairy Scary Christmas

"I'm not making bets," she answered. "I'm only taking other people's."

Summer sighed as she flipped through the names. There must be four pages of people, some of them appearing more than once. Most people had given Fern a few dollars. She saw bets of $5 and some of $10. But a few people had put bigger amounts on the contest.

"Did people bet more than once?" Summer asked.

"Some did," she shrugged. "I don't put a limit on it. If they want to come back and make another bet, I'm not going to stop them."

"Angela's on here." Summer saw the name of her neighbor twice. Once on the first page, for a small amount of $5. The second came a bit later and was for $20.

"What about Ellen Avery?"

Cousin Fern scoffed at the name.

"No way. I wouldn't have let that woman bet even if she had asked me."

Summer flipped through the pages to confirm, but she didn't see Ellen Avery's name anywhere on the page.

"She's not on here," she nodded. But another name caught her eye. A name that continued to appear, sometimes more than once, on the same page.

"Wanda Cole."

"My most frequent customer. Every time I thought she was finished, she would come back to place another bet."

Amber Crewes

Summer looked at Aunt Clara as they both ran through what this could mean.

"Who did she bet on to win?"

Cousin Fern reached an arm out and wagged her fingers at Summer, asking for the book back. She handed it over with dread building in her stomach.

"It's here in the back. Yep, just what I thought. Wanda Cole bet on herself. She thinks her house will win the decorating contest."

"She must be confident," Aunt Clara noted. "She wouldn't bet so much money on the contest if she didn't think she was going to win."

"What if she could guarantee it?" Summer asked. "What if Wanda Cole knows she'll win because she's already taken out her biggest competition?"

———

"I have to text Deputy Mason."

"Oh, you're on a texting basis now, are you?" Aunt Clara's eyebrows raised to her forehead.

"I think he's starting to trust me. I hope," she added. "I told him about Angela and her connection to Ellen. And he gave me something too. The last food Margaret ate was fruitcake. It's probably what poisoned her."

"So, who brought fruitcake to the party? We figure that out, and we have our killer."

A Hairy Scary Christmas

Summer sent Mason a text, telling him about Wanda Cole's increasingly large bets on the decorating contest. Cousin Fern complained, saying the last thing she needed was for the cops to be involved in this.

"It'll scare away my customers."

"Good," Aunt Clara nodded. "Maybe the police can shut you down permanently. Wouldn't you like a calm, quiet job? Maybe something at the diner."

"I work for myself," Fern announced. "I'm too old to have a boss."

She crossed her arms across her chest, as if ending the matter once and for all.

"We have to go," Summer said, checking her watch. "I want to be there right at the beginning. It's our best chance to see what people put down on the table."

"And what are *you* bringing?"

Summer's eyes grew wide as she realized she hadn't remembered that little detail.

"We'll stop by the cafe on the way over. I bet Evan has some day-old pastries to donate."

Clara and Fern both started to stand up, but Clara shook her head.

"Oh, no. You're staying here. We can't let this little gambling operation hit the road. It's more than likely our murderer has placed bets on this thing. What do you think they'll do to their bookie if they lose?"

Fern scowled and stood nose to nose with Aunt Clara.

151

Amber Crewes

"And what if I can help you?" she asked. "I've become very friendly with everyone in this little book. Maybe I can get some information."

It was a good point, and neither Summer nor Aunt Clara could argue with it. It felt like they were very close to figuring out who this person was. If Cousin Fern might find the last piece of crucial information, then they couldn't leave her behind.

"She has a point," Summer said, appealing to Aunt Clara. "Maybe the killer will reveal something as they're placing more bets."

"Fine," Clara sighed. "But I'm riding in the front seat."

Summer called Evan on the drive over, so he already had a box of goodies prepared when she rushed into the cafe.

"I'm sorry I can't come," he said. "Steph wasn't feeling well, so I had to send her home. So, I'll be busy prepping muffins and cinnamon rolls for all the orders tomorrow morning."

"We'll be fine," Summer smiled. "Are you sure you can spare these?"

She held up the box in her hands.

"You know I don't like to sell anything that's been out for more than a day. I can't let my standards drop on Christmas eve. Even *with* a sick baker."

"Alright. Don't work too hard."

She gave him a kiss goodbye and rushed out the door, seeing that they were already late. Any chance of seeing people place their potluck items on the table was likely out the window. Unless people were late like her.

152

A Hairy Scary Christmas

When they arrived at the church, it was easy to know where the party was. All they had to do was follow the noise of conversation and Christmas carols coming from a tiny speaker. Summer carried her box of treats down first, with Aunt Clara and Cousin Fern following behind.

"Welcome, Summer." Angela was the first person to greet her. It wasn't surprising, given how friendly Angela was that morning.

"This is so nice," she said, glancing around the room to take stock of who was there. "Is there a place I should put my food down?"

"Let me show you."

Summer glanced at Aunt Clara as Angela walked them across the room. There was a screen up along one wall, and a slideshow of images was playing. She saw Christmas light displays flipping past as those watching cheered and gasped when they saw one impressive display after another.

"You can put your food down right here."

Angela gestured to a table filled with food. One end had crock pots and casserole dishes, while the other had plates filled with Christmas cookies, brownies, and homemade chocolates. Summer had to slide a plate out of the way to find room for her box.

And there, prominently displayed on a green Christmas plate, was a fruit cake.

"And which one is yours?" Summer asked, eyeing the cake.

"Right over here."

153

Amber Crewes

To Summer's surprise, Angela gestured to the savory side of the table.

"I made my famous meatballs. They were Margaret's favorite. Well, those and Wanda's fruit cake. Make sure you don't leave here without trying it."

20

She had to squeeze Aunt Clara's arm to keep her quiet. They simply smiled and nodded at Angela until she walked away from the table of food.

"It's Wanda," Clara hissed. They scanned the room for her and instantly saw her in the back, sneaking a twenty-dollar bill to Cousin Fern.

Deputy Mason slipped through the door, dressed in street clothes. Summer was glad he hadn't arrived in uniform, since it would have been far too suspicious. This way, he could pretend he was here as a new resident of the town and not a cop.

"Be right back."

Summer gave Mason a nod, and they met at the hot chocolate station, where they each grabbed cups, pretending they truly cared about the sugary drink.

"You'll never guess what Wanda Cole brought to the party," Summer said, keeping her voice low.

155

Amber Crewes

"Wanna bet? I can go grab Fern."

Summer looked at Mason with a smile, shocked that he had made a joke. Maybe they really were becoming friends. He smiled back before spooning mini marshmallows into his drink.

"So, Wanda Cole is our fruitcake baker?" He asked. "Any proof she brought it the night before Margaret died?"

"Not exactly," Summer admitted. "But Angela told me it's her famous recipe. *And* she told me it was one of Margaret's favorites."

"Interesting. But not airtight. And what if there was more than one fruit cake that night? We need to find proof that Wanda Cole poisoned the cake. That, or we need to get a confession. Any ideas?"

Summer thought of all the money Wanda had bet on the outcome of the Decorating Contest. She clearly expected to win. How would she react if she didn't?

"Maybe we need to get a rise out of her," Summer suggested.

"What are you thinking?"

"She thinks her biggest competition is out of the way. But what if someone else wins? She has a lot riding on this. It could make her very upset."

Deputy Mason nodded, a thoughtful look on his face.

"It's worth a try. Good thinking, Summer."

"So you finally trust me?"

A Hairy Scary Christmas

She was thrilled to know Deputy Mason didn't see her as an enemy. Maybe he finally realized they were on the same team.

"Let me talk to the organizers. And when we announce the winner...just go with it."

"What are you going to do?"

Deputy Mason placed his full cup of hot chocolate on the edge of the table, clearly not intending to drink it. He looked back at her with an amused expression.

"Now it's your turn to trust me."

Summer smiled as she found Aunt Clara and Fern in the back of the room.

"That woman just gave me forty more dollars because she's so sure she's going to win," Fern said. They all knew exactly who she was talking about.

"What did Mason say?" Clara asked.

"He's going to see if he can rile her up. If he can make her upset, maybe she'll reveal something."

"If upsetting people could reveal our deepest secret, then Fern would know everything about me by now."

Just then, the commotion in the room quieted, and people took their places on the plastic chairs set up in front of the projection screen. The room was abuzz with excitement and speculation about who would win the contest. Summer glanced to the doorway and saw Deputy Mason leaning against it. He gave her the smallest of nods.

Amber Crewes

A friendly-looking man in his sixties, with a trim beard and short, white hair, made his way to the front of the room with an envelope in his hand and a small trophy.

"Hello everyone."

The room got quiet.

"I'm Councilman Elias, and I'm thrilled that so many of you decided to participate in Spring Harbor's Decorating Contest this year. First, we would be remiss if we did not take a moment to remember someone we lost too soon. The dear Margaret Edwin. As a frequent winner of this contest, we all know how much her loss means to this community. Please join me in a moment of silence to honor her."

Summer scanned the crowd, but she was standing in the back of the room. She could hear a few sniffles and see a few tissues dab at eyes, but that was it. As for Wanda Cole, she seemed to sit completely still during the sixty seconds of silence.

"Thank you. And now, the moment you've all been waiting for. The winner of this year's Spring Harbor Decorating Contest is..."

She saw Wanda Cole begin to stand up. Clearly, this woman was ready to accept her trophy. Councilman Elias hesitated a beat, and Summer saw him glance at Deputy Mason. But he pressed on and returned to the envelope in front of him.

"The winner is...Summer Snow!"

A Hairy Scary Christmas

A collective gasp was heard in the room.

"Well, now what?" Cousin Fern asked, throwing her hands up into the air. "No one bet on Summer!"

But the rest of the room wasn't exactly thinking about their bets. They were trying to determine how a woman with little more than a colorful balcony could win the Holiday Decorating Contest.

Everyone in the crowded room looked around, finally resting their eyes on Summer. But Summer was watching Wanda Cole. The woman was frozen in place, still in her half-standing position. She seemed shocked. Then Wanda looked over her shoulder and glared in Summer's direction.

"I thought you weren't competing," Angela said, her voice full of confusion. If anyone knew what Summer's decorations looked like, it was Angela. But to her credit, she managed a smile. And then she clapped, congratulating her neighbor.

"Well, go get your award," Aunt Clara whispered, nudging Summer. "And make a big show of it. You're trying to upset Wanda, remember?"

The rest of the room picked up on Angela's clapping and soon everyone was clapping as they looked at her. Summer began a slow walk down the center aisle, smiling and nodding.

"Congratulations," Councilman Elias said as she arrived at the front of the room. He handed her the envelope that announced the winner and her small trophy. Summer glanced down at the envelope and saw Wanda Cole's name on the index card. She would have won.

159

Amber Crewes

"Thank you so much," Summer said, forcing emotion into her voice. "I know my display was small, but I worked *very* hard on it."

She glanced at Wanda, remembering the glare she had given her moments ago. But now Wanda was clapping along with the rest of the room. Was she excited for her?

"I know there were big shoes to fill this year. As a newcomer to this town, I didn't get to see Margaret's incredible displays, but I hope I can continue her legacy as the new winner of the Spring Harbor Decorating Contest."

Aunt Clara cheered from the back of the room, and Cousin Fern added a whistle of celebration. They were doing everything they could to play up Summer's win and hopefully rub it in Wanda's face. But still, Wanda didn't react. She had plastered a smile on her face, and it appeared nothing would remove it.

Summer was starting to worry this plan wouldn't work. She looked to the back of the room, but Deputy Mason was no longer there. It appeared even he had given up on this.

"And I need to give a special thank you," Summer said, desperate to try one more thing. "To Wanda Cole."

Now every eye in the room turned to Wanda. She blinked at them all, startled to be called out.

"Wanda, would you please stand up?"

Maybe putting her in the spotlight would cause a reaction. It was the last thing Summer could think to try. She saw Wanda stand tentatively to her feet.

A Hairy Scary Christmas

"Wanda Cole was so gracious to allow me to participate in this contest. Just yesterday, she told me that it was too late to sign up."

Summer watched an array of expressions cross Wanda's face. There was confusion and then anger, which was quickly pushed away and replaced again with that frozen smile. Summer could tell Wanda was screaming inside, but she hadn't found a way to crack that outer shell.

"But Wanda allowed me to join you all."

Of course, this was a lie, especially since Summer was never officially a part of the contest. But no one else knew that. No one except for Wanda.

"Can everyone give Wanda Cole a round of applause, please? Without her, I never would have won."

She saw Wanda's jaw clenching in anger, pulsing as the room exploded with applause. She saw Wanda's fists clench at her sides and worried her fingernails might draw blood from pressing so hard into her palms. But still, Wanda didn't crack.

As the applause died down, Summer realized their plan had failed. They had not gotten a rise out of Wanda Cole, and they were no closer to knowing who had killed Margaret Edwin.

"Let's hear it one more time for Summer Snow," Councilman Elias said. The applause was half-hearted, with some people getting up to put their coats on even before Summer returned to her place at the back of the room.

Amber Crewes

"Well, that didn't work," Fern pointed out. Aunt Clara was more sympathetic.

"It was worth a try," she said. "Maybe she's much smarter than we think she is."

"Or maybe she didn't do it," Summer sighed. "And we're back to square one."

21

The party broke up quickly. Everyone seemed to know something weird had happened with the results, but no one was ready to make accusations. Summer heard some people asking if Councilman Elias and the judges had changed the criteria this year. Other people said they awarded a newbie to make other people in town think they could win.

Those who had brought food started to pack up their items, unplugging crock pots and trying to give away the last of the sweets so they wouldn't have to take them home. Summer saw Wanda at the table, and she took her opportunity to slide up next to her.

"Thanks again for letting me compete," Summer said. Wanda slammed the plastic cover onto her fruitcake, and Summer thought she would lash out. Finally, this was going to be the moment Wanda Cole exploded. But she only turned to Summer and smiled.

"Of course. Congratulations."

Amber Crewes

"Some of us have spent years trying to get that award," Angela said. There was an edge to her voice that made Summer wonder if she was being genuine. "How special you got it on your first try."

"Thanks," Summer said. "I feel very lucky."

"Don't forget to get your picture taken in front of the banner," Angela told her. "They'll run it in the newspaper tomorrow."

"Oh, they don't need to do that."

Summer had had quite enough of being in newspapers this week. The last thing she needed was another reason for people to hate her.

"But it's tradition," Wanda said. "Margaret started it. She said the person should be celebrated—not just the house."

It was a sweet sentiment and one Summer could see Margaret believing in. Summer remembered Margaret telling her that anytime someone complimented her hair, Margaret always told them who her hairdresser was.

"It'll only take a moment," Wanda continued.

Summer scanned the room for Aunt Clara, figuring she should tell her aunt where she was going. When she found her, she saw Clara speaking to a man in a motorcycle jacket, a helmet under his arm.

Of course, she's talking motorcycles.

"Come on, Summer. Wanda always takes the picture," Angela continued. "She's done it for years."

It felt rude to say no, so Summer nodded.

164

A Hairy Scary Christmas

"Alright. As long as it won't take long."

She saw the pleased look on Wanda's face as she scooped up the Tupperware holding her fruitcake and balanced the serving knife on top.

"Just this way."

As she watched the woman cradle her fruitcake like a precious child, Summer could only shake her head. How silly had she been to suspect Wanda Cole could murder someone over Christmas lights? The woman hadn't even protested when Summer, who wasn't part of the contest, won the award.

"Wasn't the banner at the other end of the hallway?" Summer asked.

"Just in here," Wanda said. "The lighting's good."

She realized too late that she was in trouble. Summer stepped into the small room only to have Wanda slam the door closed behind her. She dropped the fruitcake on the ground, but the sharp serving knife was now in her hand and pointed directly at Summer.

"What are you doing?" Summer asked.

"How did you win?"

Wanda lunged in Summer's direction, forcing Summer to jump backward.

"Stop it!"

"Tell me what you did. You had to know someone. Or bribe someone. What did you do?"

165

Amber Crewes

Summer scanned the room, looking for anything that could help her. It looked like they were in a small classroom, with low tables and chairs that were child sized. Summer moved backward as she knocked chairs over, obstructing Wanda's path to her. She could make a break for it if she could get herself back to the door. She just needed to keep Wanda talking.

"It's only a contest, Wanda. It's not that important."

"That's why you shouldn't have won! You're not serious about it. This is just a game to you."

Wanda threw a chair aside, clattering into a table's metal legs. Summer backed up further, feeling her heartbeat in her throat as she realized Wanda was pushing her further and further from the door. Summer had to think fast. They hadn't gotten the confession they wanted at the winner's announcement. Could she get it now?

"Is that why you did it?" Summer asked, forcing herself to stare Wanda in the eye. "Is that why you hurt Margaret?"

"Stop talking!" Wanda slashed the air with the knife, and Summer rushed backward, dropping more chairs in front of her.

"You couldn't win. You were never going to win as long as Margaret was alive."

"Enough."

"That's why you did it. You were never going to win as long as Margaret was alive. So you killed her."

"It was the only way," Wanda screamed. "She never deserved to win! But year after year, they gave her the

A Hairy Scary Christmas

award. All because she was the Mayor's wife. It was time for someone else to win. It was time for *me* to win!"

Wanda lunged forward just as Summer made a break for it. She ran hard, straight for Wanda, and shoved her arm and the knife straight into the sky.

———

The door to the classroom flew open just as Summer pushed into Wanda's arm with all her strength. Wanda fell backward, tripping over a chair that Summer had thrown on its side.

"Summer," Aunt Clara and Cousin Fern rushed into the room, closely followed by Deputy Mason. They were all there to see Wanda topple backward over the chair and land hard on the tile floor.

"Summer, step back."

Deputy Mason rushed forward, putting himself in front of Summer as Wanda scrambled to her feet. He pulled his weapon and pointed it in Wanda's direction.

"Drop your weapon, Wanda. It's time to turn yourself in."

"She did it," Summer cried from behind him. "She told me she killed Margaret. She was jealous."

"I wasn't jealous," Wanda scoffed, clearly offended by the word. "I was cheated!"

"Put it down and come in peacefully. It will go better for you."

Amber Crewes

"I could poison this whole town if I wanted to," she announced with a laugh. "No one notices the widow who lives by herself. No one suspected me."

Just then, Wanda's knees hit a chair on the ground, and she toppled over it. Deputy Mason rushed forward and pinned her arm and the weapon to the ground. He disarmed her and kicked the knife across the floor, away from her.

"Time to go," he said. He stood Wanda up just as two uniformed officers rushed into the room. They took Wanda's arms and dragged her out of the room and up to the waiting police car.

"Are you alright?" he asked Summer.

"I'm alright, but I can't believe I trusted her. How could I let her lure me into an empty room?"

"She was a good actor," Aunt Clara said. "When she didn't react to you winning, we thought she was innocent. She knew how to trick all of us."

"She's been tricking people for a long time. Not just the past week."

All eyes swung to Deputy Mason.

"That's where I was when I stepped out. I had to check on something. Do you know how Wanda Cole's first husband died?"

"I'm guessing it wasn't natural causes," Cousin Fern posited.

Deputy Mason shook his head and looked at Summer.

168

A Hairy Scary Christmas

"It was poison. Wanda Cole has killed before. We didn't solve one murder tonight, we solved two."

———

They left the room and headed upstairs, where a crowd gathered outside. Everyone at the party was now standing on the lawn, watching Wanda Cole be loaded into a police car. Summer stood next to Aunt Clara and Cousin Fern, a rush of relief washing over her.

"At least now we know what happened to Margaret. And her family has some answers."

"And you solved it just in time," Aunt Clara smiled. "Now you can turn all of your attention to Christmas dinner."

Summer groaned as she realized it was Christmas Eve. Her apartment would be full of people tomorrow, and she was hardly ready for them.

"Don't worry—I'll handle all the cooking. And Fern can bring the games. Right, Fern?"

They looked over to Cousin Fern to see her flipping through the last few pages of her small notebook, tallying something with a small pencil. Then she called out to the crowd.

"Larry, you won! You pegged Wanda Cole as the murderer. Come see me for your winnings."

22

"Be careful with that," Clara said, leaning over the ham as Evan pulled a knife through the meat. "We spent all day on it."

"And now it's your turn to relax," Evan chuckled. "You and Summer have been in the kitchen for hours—go take a break."

"Break and Aunt Clara don't usually go in the same sentence," Summer laughed. She sipped her wine before handing a fresh glass to Clara.

"Why don't you go make sure Cousin Fern isn't swindling anyone out of their money?"

"Good idea," Clara said. She took the wine and made a bee-line for Cousin Fern, who was waving a pack of cards in front of Alex and Carl.

Summer's apartment was a buzz of energy. Christmas music played through the house while her guests perched around her small living room and kitchen, chatting and

171

Amber Crewes

snacking. Barney and Betty ran from person to person, begging until someone gave in and fed them something.

"I don't think we have enough chairs," Misty said, as she and Deputy Mason set the table. She saw Misty scan the room, counting heads.

"We can use the bench by the door," Summer said. "And don't forget Mrs. Beesley's joining us for dessert."

The oven beeped and Summer quickly turned off the offensive sound. Then she pulled the green bean casserole and mashed potatoes from the oven, setting them on her counter.

"We have *way* too much food," she laughed. "Anyone else you want to invite?"

"I don't think they would fit," Evan responded. "I'm amazed you squeezed this many people in here already."

Alex came to the kitchen to refill her wine glass, patting Betty on the head as she walked by her.

"I thought you might bring this new mystery guy of yours," Summer teased. "Did he already have plans for Christmas?"

"Sadly, he was busy today," Alex smirked. "So I guess the mystery continues."

"Wait a minute, you promised to give me more info. Isn't that why I cut your hair for free?"

"I thought you didn't want any money." Alex shrugged her shoulders nonchalantly, brushing this aside.

"But I *do* want information. Who is this guy? Where did you meet him? Are you happy?"

172

A Hairy Scary Christmas

"She always needs a mystery to solve, doesn't she?" Alex said, glancing at Evan, who was still hard at work on the ham.

"She's not happy without one," he agreed.

"No fair. Now you two are ganging up on me."

Evan smiled at Summer and wrapped an arm around her shoulder, giving her a side-hug.

"Oh! Your present," Alex said. She rushed over to the tree and came back with a small box. It was wrapped in red paper, complete with dogs wearing Santa hats.

"So cute!" Summer cooed. She tore open the present to reveal a small, flat box. When she removed the top, she saw a Christmas ornament inside with the press of a dog's paw print right in the middle.

"Is this Barney's paw print?"

"It is. We made them one of the nights I was dog-sitting. I have one for Betty, too."

Summer wrapped Alex in a hug.

"Thank you. I love it."

"This food smells so good," Alex said as they released from their hug. "Can we eat it already?"

Summer surveyed the steaming dishes in front of them and the neatly sliced ham. She quickly ran through the menu in her head and found that everything was accounted for.

"Alright everyone, the food's ready."

Amber Crewes

Friends and family descended on the food, filling their plates with all the smells of Christmas. They barely fit around the table, but they managed to squeeze in. Summer had brought home the flimsy folding table from the salon to add to her small dining table. But the cramped quarters only added to the charm. They bumped elbows and talked over each other, enjoying every second.

And, of course, the conversation eventually turned to Wanda Cole and her arrest.

"That's right," Mason nodded. "She made a full confession to both crimes. Sheriff Brady's pretty happy to get that cold case off his desk."

"Maybe he'll finally see that Summer is here to help him," Misty suggested, but Summer was skeptical. She was grateful she had won over Deputy Mason, but her history with Brady was far longer. He was a harder nut to crack.

"Imagine being so lonely that you would kill someone over Christmas lights," Alex mused. "I'm glad that's not me."

"Me too," Misty agreed.

"Do you think Ellen Avery will apologize?" Evan asked. "She was so sure the Mayor was somehow responsible for this. But turns out he had nothing to do with it."

"I want to know if he'll keep things going with that assistant of his," Cousin Fern chimed in. "Anyone want to bet on it?"

The whole table groaned and then erupted in laughter at Fern's boldness.

A Hairy Scary Christmas

"Alright, everyone, I have an announcement to make."

Carl stood up from the table, drawing everyone's eye. They had finished most of their meal, with some people indulging in second helpings, while others groaned about how full they were. The group got quiet as they looked at Carl.

"I thought you'd never get around to it," Aunt Clara said. "Is it here? Is it outside?"

She pushed away from the table and squeezed between the couch and people's folding chairs to make her way to the balcony. A chill rushed through the apartment as Clara opened the door and went outside to peek out to the parking lot.

Carl put a finger to his mouth for the rest of the table and then snuck forward so he was standing near the open sliding door.

"Where is it?" Clara asked as she bent over the Christmas-light-clad railing. Losing patience, she turned back to look into the apartment. There, Carl was down on one knee with a small box in his hand.

"Carl," she gasped. A hand rushed to Clara's mouth as she stepped back inside. Summer found Evan's hand and squeezed it, overcome with the romance of the moment.

"Clara, you're a wild and crazy trip, and I never want it to end. Will you marry me?"

"Yes!"

Clara rushed forward to hold out her left hand. He placed a shiny ring on her finger before standing up to swoop her

Amber Crewes

into a kiss. The whole dinner table clapped and cheered for the happy couple.

"This was a surprise," Clara said, brushing tears from her eyes. "Did any of you know about this?"

She turned to everyone at the table, who all shook their heads. Everyone except for Cousin Fern.

"Wait a minute," Aunt Clara said. "You were in on it?"

"Do you really think I'd give him money to let you risk your life on a motorcycle? I told Carl there were better things to spend his money on."

She glanced down at Aunt Clara's finger, where the diamond sparkled among the Christmas lights.

"I should have known," Clara said, shaking her head. "You've always been a troublemaker. And I love you for it."

Everyone at the table stood up to hug and congratulate the couple. Summer pulled Aunt Clara into a tight hug.

"I'm so happy for you," she said. "Now, maybe we can put our energy into planning a wedding instead of solving crimes."

"Let's hope," Clara nodded. "We could use some quiet around here."

One of Alex's favorite Christmas songs began to play, and she rushed over to the speaker to turn up the volume. She started singing, and soon everyone else joined in. Summer put an arm around Evan's waist, and the two of them swayed together, playfully singing.

176

A Hairy Scary Christmas

"Let's get a picture," Deputy Mason suggested. "Everyone gather on the balcony."

"The award-winning balcony, you mean," Summer laughed.

"Exactly. Everyone gather in front of Spring Harbor's best Christmas decorations."

The group squeezed together on the balcony, with Alex even coaxing the dogs into the picture. Mason stood against the back of the couch, trying to back up enough to fit everyone in the frame.

"Okay, squeeze in," he said. "Now say 'Christmas Lights'."

"Christmas Lights!"

The End

Afterword

Thank you for reading *A Hairy Scary Christmas*. I really hope you enjoyed reading it as much as I had writing it!

If you have a minute, please consider leaving a review on Amazon, GoodReads and/or Bookbub.

Many thanks in advance for your support!

A Grim Trim in a Gym

Sneak Peek

Sneak Peek

"I can't believe you convinced me to do this," Summer said.

She looked around as half a dozen women removed their coats and shoes, revealing trendy leggings and colorful tops.

"It will be fun," Alex insisted. "It's part of our New Year's resolution."

"Aren't we supposed to make those individually?" Summer asked.

She hung her coat on one of the hangers and handed another to Alex. They were in 'Stretch and Strength', Spring Harbor's yoga studio. Summer had never been very athletic, so the thought of a yoga class wasn't exactly her idea of a good time. But her best friend was nothing if not persuasive.

"We can have a joint resolution, can't we?"

Amber Crewes

Alex was carefully looking around the room, almost like she was taking stock of everyone attending this class. Summer slipped off her shoes.

"It's not like you gave me a choice," she said. "You signed me up for a one-month trial without even asking me."

"It's good for you," she shrugged.

They walked to the front desk to check in, where a young woman with blonde hair piled on top of her head beamed at them.

"Welcome to 'Stretch and Strength'. Is this your first time with us?"

"Sure is," Alex said. "We're here for a class with Everly."

"Yes, she's the owner of this place. She's *the best* teacher. You won't be disappointed."

"And just out of curiosity, which one *is* Everly?" Alex asked. She scanned the studio behind the girl, looking intently at each woman stretching on a yoga mat.

"She's just over there."

The girl at the desk pointed behind Alex to a corner of the studio where some merchandise was displayed. Summer followed her gaze and saw a pretty, thin woman with long blonde hair. She was speaking to a man who was nearly twice her size, towering over her with bulging muscles that stretched the sleeves of his t-shirt. Summer saw annoyance on Everly's face, and a scowl of anger on the man's. Were they arguing?

"Thank you," Alex said.

A Grim Trim in a Gym

She grabbed Summer and pushed her back toward the coat rack, away from the yoga studio.

"Alright, we can go."

"Go? What do you mean? We haven't taken the class yet."

"We're not here to take the class," Alex whispered. "We're here to see Everly. Now that we've seen her, we can go."

"Alex, that's not an explanation," Summer said. "Who is Everly?"

Her friend continued pulling their coats from the rack, trying to be discreet and failing miserably.

"My boyfriend's ex. Apparently, they were pretty serious."

Summer felt instantly embarrassed, shocked to know Alex had dragged her along to spy on someone.

"Alex, you can't just creep on people like that. And we certainly can't bail on the class *now*. They'll think we're weird."

"Who cares," Alex shrugged. "We'll just say yoga isn't for us."

"Hi there, I hear it's your first class with us today."

They looked up to see Everly crossing toward them, a huge smile on her face. Summer's stomach dropped as she realized Everly had caught them trying to leave.

"Sorry, I just realized I have to go," Alex said. "I remembered...I don't like yoga."

Summer glanced at her, trying to tell her friend to cool it,

185

but Alex seemed far too flustered. It was out of character for Alex. She must really like this new boyfriend...

"Oh, but you should stay," she insisted. "I know starting something new can be intimidating, but you're not the only new people in the class. And I'll offer modifications throughout our poses to make things easier or more challenging based on your fitness level. I think you'll really like it."

She looked to be about their age, and Summer quickly liked her. She had a welcoming, kind presence that she knew must serve her well as a business owner.

Summer looked at Alex, ready to take the lead from her friend. But before Alex could answer, the girl from the desk returned, carrying two yoga mats.

"I grabbed some mats for you," she said. "I can show you where to set them up if you'd like."

It seemed they were past the point of no return. Alex removed her coat with a sigh and returned it to the rack, resolved to stay. Then she and Summer followed the girl into the studio.

"Now you'll have more time to watch her," Summer said, trying to bolster Alex up, but her friend looked at her with distress.

"I really do hate yoga," Alex grumbled.

―――

Summer enjoyed the class more than she thought. Even Alex seemed to like it, telling her it was much different from

A Grim Trim in a Gym

the last class she tried. But it didn't stop them from wanting to rush out of there. Summer was still feeling strange about spying on Everly on Alex's behalf, so she rolled up the borrowed mat as quickly as possible.

"How did you like it?"

Everly was suddenly standing over them, smiling. She looked like she had hardly broken a sweat, but Summer's own reflection in the mirror was red and flushed.

"Challenging," Summer said. "I liked it."

She stood up and handed the yoga mat to Everly. She waited as Alex had a bit more trouble with her mat, handing it over more folded than rolled.

"And you?" Everly asked.

Alex kept her gaze on her feet as she talked to her.

"Good. Great."

We made it, Summer thought. *Now, let's get out of here so we can never come back.*

"You know, you look so familiar."

Summer froze as Everly stared at Alex.

"Really? I guess I have one of those faces," Alex said.

Alex tried to walk away, but Everly wasn't ready to let her go.

"Wait...are you Colin's new girlfriend?"

Summer's stomach flipped at this, knowing this could go in a million different directions. She had no idea if Everly and

Amber Crewes

Alex's boyfriend, who she had just learned was named Colin, had ended on positive terms.

"Oh, you know Colin?" Alex asked, feigning ignorance.

Everly's face broke out in a grin, and Summer finally let out the breath she was holding.

"I knew that was you," she said. "I told Colin he looks so happy these days. And do you know what he told me? He said you're the reason. How sweet is that?"

"He said that?" Alex asked. It was clear she was touched by this.

"Definitely. I'm so happy for him. Even though we're not together anymore, I still care for him, you know?"

Everly stopped then and put her hand out, touching Alex's elbow ever so lightly.

"Not romantically, of course," she assured her. "Not that it would matter. Colin only has eyes for you these days."

Something bothered Summer, and she jumped into the conversation, breaking up all Everly's compliments.

"How did you recognize Alex?" she asked. Summer hadn't seen any pictures of Alex and her new boyfriend on social media. She hadn't even seen the new boyfriend in public yet. So how had Everly seen them?

"Oh, I saw Colin at the gym the other day."

"He does yoga?" Summer asked, looking to Alex for confirmation, but both women shook their heads.

"No, not yoga," Alex said.

A Grim Trim in a Gym

"Weightlifting is more his style," Everly continued. "He works out at Spring Harbor Fitness, which is my gym, too. As much as I love yoga, I've got to get some cardio and weights in there, too, you know? Plus, it's fun to see everyone from town and say hello. It's a very social place."

"He loves that place," Alex said, confirming that Colin spent time there.

"Me too. Such a great community of people. Anyway, after I told him how happy he seemed, he showed me a picture of you. In a horse-drawn carriage, I think?"

Alex nodded, and her eyes went soft at the memory.

"That was New Year's Eve," she said.

Summer was surprised Alex hadn't told her about something like a horse-drawn carriage on New Year's Eve. And why was it only today that she finally learned the man's name? She was starting to question why Alex was keeping so many details from her. Why did Colin's ex-girlfriend know more about their relationship than Summer did?

"I still haven't met him," Summer said. "I was starting to think Alex was making him up."

Alex rolled her eyes at Summer as Everly laughed.

"He's real," Everly said. "And he's a good guy. I'm happy for you both."

Everly smiled sweetly at Alex, and she returned the favor.

"Thanks again for the class," Summer said.

Amber Crewes

"Of course. Come back anytime. We love having new faces here."

"We will," Alex said, surprising Summer. But then she remembered all the nice things Everly said about her. She didn't blame Alex for wanting to return for more of the same.

"She's nice," Alex whispered as they put their coats back on, bundling up for the cold January air.

"She is," Summer agreed. "But next time you take me along to stalk someone, could you at least give me a heads up?"

"Now, what would be the fun in that?" Alex said with a smirk.

———

You can order your copy of **A Grim Trim in a Gym** at any good online retailer.

A SPRING HARBOR COZY MYSTERY 9

A GRiM TRiM in a GYM

AMBER CREWES

Newsletter Signup

Want **FREE** COPIES OF FUTURE **AMBER CREWES** BOOKS, FIRST NOTIFICATION OF NEW RELEASES, CONTESTS AND GIVEAWAYS?

GO TO THE LINK BELOW TO SIGN UP TO THE NEWSLETTER!

www.AmberCrewes.com/cozylist

Made in United States
Troutdale, OR
12/21/2024

27144263R00116